DEDICATION

For Niall and my parents Joyce and George.

No Strings Attached: Tales of the Frixians

Angela Timms

ACKNOWLEDGMENTS

I would like to thank The Vale of Rheidol Railway and The Dr Who Exhibition. With special thanks to The Doctor for allowing us to borrow the TARDIS.

1 THE WEAVER OF DREAMS

Wizel looked around the cave. He was a small, one foot tall, wizened old man with pointy ears and scant hair. His brown wool jerkin was tied with a bit of twine and hung over his baggy cream trousers which in turn were tucked into his brown cloth boots. He was supposed to be alone. Or he thought he was. He didn't see Rak above him, lurking in the shadows. Rak looked like him, similarly skinny but dressed in black, with black hair and much, much younger. Rak's long sinuous fingers wrapped around the rocks which allowed him to cling precariously to a nearby flat wall while he stared down at the bald head of the imp with the long pointed nose and long rheumy fingers. Those fingers were knotted like old sticks and as he tried to tie up a parcel with brown string Wizel made little grunting noises as the paper and string slipped away from him.

Rak thought about helping but that would mean that Wizel would find out he was there and he didn't want that. Wizel had something he wanted and once he was gone he would climb down and get it And a few other things for his trouble. He'd already looked around the room at the eclectic mix of old furniture and fascinating objects. He had no idea what they were but they were either valuable or useful, he couldn't decide which. It wouldn't matter, he'd find a use for them once the old one went to bed.

Time passed and Rak's fingers began to ache and he did feel slightly dizzy from hanging almost upside down. He could hear Wizel humming but there was something more in the sound, words he couldn't understand woven into the humming. He realized too late that Wizel was casting a spell and as he fell to the ground with a thump his dulling mind thought. "Oh blast!". That was as much as he could manage before it all went dark.

Wizel looked down at the Raksasi. It was still only a foot tall but had become black and scaly as the image of an imp like Wizel faded away. The magic that had created the illusion of the creature being an imp was gone, the spell broken. The creature was frozen in a hideous pose with its fingers still gripping empty air where the rocks had been before Wizel had removed them magically from his grip and frozen him.

Rak's skin was now leathery where it wasn't scaly, black, his wings folded under a thick carapace like a bug's wing. Useless now of course as the creature lay frozen, its unseeing eyes still open, its mouth open in its last comment before it had slid into a forced unconsciousness.

Wizel looked down at the creature and poked it with his pointy boot. "Are you dead? No, you can't be dead, I didn't use that spell. Ok you are unconscious so you aren't just being rude. Are you unconscious?" Rak couldn't answer.

Wizel looked down again and went to the fire and found the poker and gave the Raksasi a firm poke in what he estimated would be the ribs if they had ribs. Nothing happened.

Wizel took out a gnarled old wand from the long thin leather pouch he kept it in and waved it above the prone creature and whispered ancient words. He pulled a misty stream from the creature's head which became solid and hung in the air, a sheet of mist with words forming on it.

Wizel read the words and grunted. "So, you want to steal from me do you? Well, you will not. You will now go and never return. In fact you will never remember you were here and you will not remember what you wanted."

He waved his wand and the creature disappeared with a slight popping noise and the smell of violets. Wizel smiled, he liked the violet smell, it was his own personal addition to his magic.

He rubbed his pointy chin with his gnarly fingers. "Darn it, the Red Queen won't like this. Raksasi in the Queendom. That is bad, that is really bad. Something bad is going on and I'm far too old to be a hero again and I bet I get mixed up in all this. I bet the Queen will have something to say. Perhaps one last adventure for me then before I completely retire. Although I am already supposed to be retired." He spoke to the empty air.

He looked along his bookcase which was stuffed full of tatty paperback novels he had stolen from Earth gathered on his visits. "Well is this how a great adventure starts? At least I didn't have my village burnt, my family murdered and a huge chip placed firmly on my muscly shoulders."

He fluffed himself up and looked in the mirror as an elderly weedy reflection looked back and shattered his mental illusion. "Oh well, never mind. I will have to do."

He went to a big dark wood chest and pulled open the bottom drawer. He reached inside and pulled out a flat black disc with a red label and a hole in the middle. "I still have it. Silly creature failed. I still hold it in my hands and now I have remembered it. I don't know how I forgot it. It was so important wasn't it? I must be getting very, very old."

Wizel looked down at the 78" record and smiled to himself. "Yes, I still have it but shame I don't still have "it"."

There was a crack of thunder and a flash of red light and Wizel and the record disappeared.

The Red Queen sat on her ebony throne. Her long red curls cascaded down over her blood red velvet dress. She looked up when Wizel appeared on the thick red carpet in front of her in her gold embellished throne room.

She almost smiled as Wizel found his feet, saw her and then fell over backwards as he realized where he was.

A small white rabbit, wearing a red velvet squires' livery with the Queen's flaming unicorn on it grabbed a bowl which held floating candles and threw the contents over Wizel who was just coming around anyway and trying to stand up. Wizel then jumped up with a squeal and glared at the unfortunate creature who cowered, muttering. "Please don't turn me into anything else, I've only just got used to being a rabbit. I was just trying to help."

Wizel stood up, the water dripping from his pointed nose and was about to speak but the Red Queen cut him off by raising her hand. "Wizel, you have brought it to us? I thank you. You have served us well. You will be rewarded. Now you must do what must be done, one last adventure. Like I told you all those years ago when you first brought it back. That is old magic you are holding. The magic of dreams bound into a black disc which came from the Earth place. The music has power, the song chosen to wake the dreaming one. She must now return to their world. The time is right. Take it and play it on their music box and make the dragon wake up. It is the time."

Wizel bowed his head and he could feel his knees knocking together. He wasn't sure if it was the chill of the water which was running down his back and neck or pure terror at standing in front of the most scary woman he had ever met. Or perhaps the thought of crossing the realms and entering the "World of Men" was what scared him. It was indeed a truly terrifying thought even though he had done it many times before. He decided it was the Queen mostly and tried to find his courage to look up again.

The Red Queen cleared her throat. "We will be expecting you to do your duty again. You must take the black disc to the land of men as it will restore magic to their world."

Wizel spoke without thinking and immediately bit his tongue. "Why?" In his mind they were mortals and their world without magic was their world. "Many creatures will be awoken or able to return if "she" is awoken."

It took a mere moment for all the thoughts of the old times where elves and pixies played in the ancient woodlands to flood through his tiny head. It took only a further moment before a dark shadow crept over his mind's eye as he saw the mechanized glass and stone world where magic was for stories and the old fears and respects were buried. "What space does mankind have for old fears of strange creatures in the horrors of the man created warlike world? Where will the mystic creatures fit in amongst a world where everything has to be scientifically explained. Where does faith fit in where people have to know, have to have everything proven and documented. Of course absolute proof takes out the element of the wondrous and infinite."

The Queen smiled to herself and drew herself up to her full height on the throne. "Would you dare to question me? You will do as you are told."

Wizel bowed several times as low as he could and nearly fell over. Over and over again he declared. "Your wish is my command. Your wish is my command."

The Queen smiled a cold smile. "Yes, I know. I understand your reservations and in part share them but it must be."

The rabbit had backed away and was cowering behind a chair which was one of a line of chairs set out for their official occupiers on meeting days. They were all empty. The room was empty other than the Queen, Wizel and the rabbit. The rabbit was nearly hiding himself, it took all his courage to stay standing in front of the Queen. The rabbit at that point moved from cowering to actually trying to crawl under a chair. All Wizel could see were a pair of ears which were shaking and the bob of a tail which didn't quite fit behind the chair. It was a very small chair, made for the Queen's court of Fey. These were of course tiny when they chose to be and huge when they wanted to be. For the sake of many thousands of chairs which were solid gold the Queen preferred them to appear before her as tiny.

Wizel looked around the room, looking for something he could use to change the subject but then his eyes were drawn back to the wand which lay across the Queen's lap. He knew what that wand could do and he knew she was not afraid to use it.

Wizel shut his eyes as he saw the Red Queen raise her wand. He felt the ground shift and the softness of the carpet was replaced by a slightly deeper softness and the smell of damp loam from the woodland floor.

He opened his eyes, first one and then the other. It was dark, not pitch black, illuminated by the soft twinkling of a myriad of stars which created a canopy over his head. He could make out some of the constellations, the plough, Orion and others. He could clearly see them through the circular gap in the tree canopy. The trees were around him, not above making a round disc of stars.

He was also standing in a circle of tree stumps within the circle of evergreen living trees.

The clearing was part of a garden to the side of a farmhouse.

To his right, between the garden and the house there was a bubbling brook which tumbled down a small waterfall, slipped gurgling under a bridge made of wooden half fencing posts before it rushed off into the darkness under the road below.

He could hear birds singing and the sound of sheep. Somewhere a cockerel crowed and he knew he was on Earth. He took a deep breath. Not that he had expected the Queen's spell to fail but with magic there was always the possibility, however slight and however powerful you are. He took a deep breath and climbed up and sat on the stump which was a little taller than him. He still held the record which was as big as he was and swiftly slipped it into a bag he had in his pocket with great care. The bag shrank itself and the record to a small size so that he could carry it easily. He then began to worry about the horrible things that could happen to him if he did break it and then he spent more moments trying to forget about those thoughts

He looked around and in the shadows something moved. Something black, velvety and deadly. He knew what cats were. Previous visits to Earth had provided a few very close shaves with a furry feline and he had no intention of getting caught this time either. He saw her emerald eyes and sharp claws and wicked natural intent and he knew if she caught him it would be all over for him. He took his wand and waved it and the resulting flash meant that the cat gave a surprised yowl and disappeared off back into the shadows.

Wizel froze as he heard a voice. It was a language he had not heard for many years, a voice he could understand. It was like a sheep bleat but not quite the same. It was a fairy sound. It was one that he had known from the grey mists of time and a creature who had always served his kind as a loyal mount and friend. He heard a goat.

He followed the sound and crossed the bridge. When

he got to the other side of the stream he could clearly see the farmhouse which was feet away, its lights dark, its white wall glowing in the moonlight under the trees and the huge ancient fuchsia bush which was also as big as a tree. The walkway down the side of the house was filled with slushy rotting leaves. Behind the house was a steep bank so he climbed it. It was difficult to start with as the soil was quite loose.

Further up the hill he could see the dark shadows of two sheds. They too were in darkness. To the right of them there was a grey stone building with three doors. He tried to move quietly but even his tiny feet made a noise in the layers of leaves and twigs. He dived for cover at the sound that came from this building. The hounds of hell were coming to get him. They howled as they smelt something strange in their territory. The sound echoed in the stillness of the night waking animals and resonating around the valley. It was an ancient sound that was primal and wild. He was certain the hounds would come and get him but as they fell silent his rational thought told him that the doors were shut and he was quite safe as they were locked away. They had obviously sensed his otherworldly presence which had unnerved them.

Wizel picked himself up from the dark corner he had been hiding in, brushed the leaves off of his tattered brown wool tunic and smoothed his trousers down.

He smoothed his hair and stood up straight, gathering his thoughts.

"Creatures of the Wolfkind, I am not of your realm. I will not hurt you if you will not hurt me." He smiled as he felt he had soothed them and calmed them. He didn't like harming or upsetting any animal.

He jumped as one of them answered him back. "I am Jackeran of the Ukerajkus, Keeper of the Light for Wolfkind. I know you for what you are and you are welcome in our lands. I and my canine friends will not harm you."

Wizel looked surprised as an answer was not what he was expecting. He had heard of Jackeran. The wolf spirit could inhabit a wolf or dog to give itself a presence in different realms. "Great Wolf of the North. Why are you here and how are you here?"

Jackeran laughed a gutteral woofy sort of a laugh. "I am tired of the politics of the races. I am here because I can choose where I want to be. I wish no more than to be a faithful hound, to be fed on time and to be a loyal dog. I would not be a man again for all the dog food in Morrisons. The question is why are you here and where are you going? To see the goats? You better not be intending to harm them. I would not allow that."

Wizel shifted his weight. He was feeling increasingly less secure as he knew that the doors of the dog kennel would not hold Jackeran if he chose to break them down. "It is a secret."

Jackeran growled slightly. "You carry hope in your bag. Why do you not trust me with your secret?"

Wizel jumped. "How do you know?

Jack spoke quietly, his voice like velvet. "Fool, I am old, the world is young and what you hold in your bag is old magic. I can smell it."

Wizel looked surprised. He was trying to stop his legs from shaking. "It is only a record, an old record and not as old as you are saying."

Jack snuffled the cage bars and thought about breaking them. He frowned but he sat down. "The magic is old. The record is young. One does not preclude the other. The goats will not help you you know. They serve the Frixian in the house and they will not let you take anything from here. Nor will the mistress and master."

Wizel grunted. "You know too much and you assume too much or you are trying to make me tell you. What I have to do is important. I cannot let them stop me but that is not a threat. If they know what I am doing they will want to help me surely."

Jack cocked his head to one side. "Well if it wasn't such a secret that might be the truth. Speak your truth and you may get some help."

Wizel looked around nervously. "I assumed that I had to do a great quest and travel many miles across dangerous terrain."

Jack laughed which ended up as a half bark, half laugh. "Fool, you read too much. You need to play that record, see I know your secret. That is all you need to do. Are you a great warrior? I don't think so. So the task you are set must suit what you can do. It is an old record but I know that mistress has a record player that is quite old and may well be able to play it."

Wizel looked into the darkness. "So how do I get it played? It must be played."

Jack nodded his big hairy German Shepherd head somewhere in the darkness of the kennel. "Indeed it must so put it in that shed you can see. There is a silver metal barrel with other records in it. Put it on top of the others and when you are finished you must go and find the Frixians who live in the house, Widget and Gadget. They will help you. You will find them in the living room."

Wizel stood outside the dog kennel in the moonlight. The scent of Geraniums filled his senses. The loamy earth under his feet was soft and rutted with old footprints and paw prints.

He didn't know if the humans in the house would be awake although probably not as it was the early hours of the morning and that made him cautious. He couldn't hear anything but that didn't mean that they weren't awake so he walked down the hill very carefully. Step by step, his feet making very little sound as they came into contact with the soil, grass and the rock which protruded between the grass. He could see where he was going, now that he was out of the trees the moonlight lit his way. He almost relaxed before the light outside the house came on. He had been found by the sensor and the hillside lit up. Without thinking he dived sideways and landed in a patch of stinging nettles. The tingling sensation crawled over any part of his body that wasn't covered by clothes and he swore, knowing that he would now feel that horrible sensation for hours. He also had to lay there, waiting for the light to go out and that was torture. It didn't take long, the light went out and he leapt up. Of course that set the light off again and he dived back into the nettles. Again the stinging sensation found all the parts of his skin that had been missed the last time and again he lay there, thinking about what had happened until he worked it out.

The house was dark and quiet. Wizel guessed that they would be sleeping upstairs so after cautiously peering in through the cat flap he climbed through it and emerged onto the tiled floor of what looked like a kitchen diner.

His little feet didn't make much sound as he tip toed to the first step which was as tall as he was. He stood on his tip toes and reached up. He grabbed the metal edge strip using it to pull himself up onto the next step. One foot on top and pulled himself up. He then did the same up onto the next step. Now rather out of breath but triumphant he stood on the top of the two steps and looked around the room. It was near to pitch black, the only glow coming from electric equipment in the corner, the television and DVD player. It did light his way across the floor, past the dining table and chairs and past the dark wood kitchen. He wasn't sure if he was going the right way but as the main part of the house was that way and there didn't seem to be another way but he hoped he was right. There didn't seem to be a record player in the room he was in, so next door it would have to be.

More stairs. This time going down. He looked down the steps and sighed. He crouched down, put a hand on the top step, then the other and then lowered himself down. Then he did the same and then the same again.

At the bottom of the stairs he stopped. The door was shut. He gave it a push and sighed with relief as the door wasn't locked or latched and although it was heavy he managed to open it when he pushed with all his strength.

The room beyond was dark, very dark. As he stepped through the slightly open door then froze as a voice made him jump. "What are you doing here imp?"

Wizel bowed to the three foot tall creature who stood in front of him. She was three times his height and nearly as tall as a kitchen cabinet. Her hair was long, black and curly. Her pointed ears protruded from her curls. "Greetings oh guardian of the house. I have come to fulfil a task I was given by the Red Queen. Jackeran said you might be able to help me."

The creature physically shuddered. "If Her Majesty wishes it then we will help. I can feel this is true, her mark is with you. So what do we have to do? How can we help?"

Wizel smiled and he relaxed. "I came with a record that has been kept for many years. It must be played now. It is a song which was recorded by a human called Nat King Cole many years ago but there is something in the words and music which will wake up the Weaver of Dreams. She is important as mankind needs to dream, if mankind can dream again of the old magic then magic and magical creatures will return to the world. The darkness of the Goblians and other wicked creatures have grown strong here. We hope that having good magical dreams will help to fight them off."

Widget looked as confused as a material faced puppet could look, she tilted her head to the side. "So, who are you? Tell me what we need to do next?"

Wizel bowed again. "I am sorry, I am forgetting all my manners in my haste. I am Wizel, currently in the service of the Red Queen and formerly of the Purple Watch and various other honorary and other more robust titles that I will not bore you with. May I ask who you are?"

Widget curtseyed gracefully, or rather as gracefully as a stuffed puppet who hadn't been in that body long can. "I am Stellastar Widget, Daughter of the Frixian Realm and Custodian and Guardian of the TAVERN."

Wizel had heard of the TAVERNS. They had long been the transport of the Peacekeepers and the Truth Masters but he knew from his history and rumours that they had been lost for many years. He had no reason to doubt her, she looked sincere but he was surprised.

Widget looked sad. "How will playing the record and bringing dreams back help? Mankind is selfish and opinionated and disbelieves what is true just because they can. They are more interested in owning the latest Audi from the catalogue than caring about their world unless it suits them to make them feel good or to balance the bad that they do. You never know I suppose, bringing back dreams may bring a change."

Wizel coughed. "So you don't like mankind much?"

Widget smiled slightly. "I don't like what mankind has done to such and beautiful and magical world. I don't like it that mankind no longer fears the dark or respects nature's ability to fight back."

Wizel smiled to himself, a sympathetic smile. "If the music is played and magic returns to this realm then all the Old Ways will return too. Magic will be real again and no amount of using group disbelief will banish it again."

Widget smiled a wistful smile. "We must play the record then."

In the darkness someone woke, the mistress of the house. She looked around the darkened room and felt something she had not felt for a very long time. She could smell blackcurrants and there was a strange light in the room as three tall white people, a woman, a man and an older man with a very long beard walked through the wall beside her bed and stepped towards her.

She smiled, memories flooding back of her childhood when they had visited her before. "Am I dreaming?" She whispered.

They bowed their heads and the first of them spoke. She was very feminine and held her elegant long limbs with poise. Her long white hair tumbled down her back and over her the shoulders of her long gown swaying gently as she raised her hands reassuringly. "Are you sleeping?"

The woman looked up into the visitor's face. There was a gentle light in her visitor's eyes as she felt reassured. "I was. Am I sleeping? Am I dreaming?"

All three smiled. The woman. The man with a long beard and matching robes who stood beside her and the older man who stood behind them. Then the younger man spoke. "Do you remember us?"

The woman nodded her head. "It has been years. Was I dreaming then? Am I dreaming now?"

The younger man smiled kindly. "In this world there is a boundary between dream, illusion and reality. Although we are not what you would call real as in we have physical bodies, we exist, and we are. This is important. We need you to do something for the world and it is a very simple something. We need you to go to your shed and open your parents' record tin and bring the top record back to the house. We would then like you to play the record. It is important. Tomorrow we need you to do something else. We would like you to go to your small barn, the one you made into the TAVERN and pick up the key that your father used to own, the big old fashioned one and put it back on its hook. We must go now but please do these things for us."

Angel sat on the side of her bed. Her bare feet touched the cold wood beneath her feet. She slipped her feet into her slippers and slipped on her silken gown before walking to the door in the moonlight. To get to the stairs she walked through bedroom turned into the walk in wardrobe, shut the door and put the light on.

The stairs creaked slightly as she walked down. The narrow stairway as always commanding concentration as there had been a couple of times that she had missed a step and nearly fallen. When she was on the bottom step she pushed the door open at the bottom and stepped down onto the stone multi coloured floor of the room below.

Wizel and Widget ran into the back kitchen when they heard footsteps so by the time the woman got to the door they were long gone. They watched from the back kitchen, through the serving hatch and saw her open the front door, slip on some boots and go outside, leaving the internal door open.

The woman stepped out into the chilled moonlight night which bathed her face in a mystical glow. Her black hair a stark contrast to her pale skin, her hazel eyes reflecting a slight golden tint. She looked around, sensing the magic that was in the air and smelling the night air. She took a deep breath, breathing it deep into her lungs so that she could feel the chill. She walked slowly and carefully as if she was in a dream, trying to work out if she was awake or not. It was hard to tell as the whole place looked mystical. She walked across the stone balcony outside the house. The rough grey concrete seemed to sparkle as the quartz in the stone caught the moonlight. The ivy and bushes had overgrown and the slightly rusty gate took a little effort to open. She lifted the latch and opened the metal gate which was partially overgrown. She had often looked down at the ball shaped stones which protruded from the concrete the other side of the gate and wondered why. They didn't make it less slippery, on the contrary she had often wondered if they made it worse but there they were embedded in concrete, a slab of stone which ended with a definite step out on to the grass. In contrast the grass was soft and springy underfoot and she kept to the edges of the track up the hill beside the house where it grew undamaged by the quad bike and walked slowly up the hill. The night was chilled, cloudless and the moon bright enough for her not to need a torch as she was very used to the hill in the evening. The dim light was enough.

She followed the small hedge on top of a mound on her left hand side until it opened up between the two posts which had long since had their gate removed. Beyond this it opened up into an odd shape created by previous plans by previous owners where trees and shrubs had been planted which had grown beyond their original size and at least one path which had been steps up the side of the hill went nowhere. To her right the metal shed where the animal food was stored was silhouetted by the moon beyond. It was most of the way across the sky so she knew that the hour was late. She had mastered knowing the time during the day by the sun but she hadn't quite worked out the night movements of the moon. The trees beyond the shed clung to the hill and seemed skeletal at that time of the year testament to the winter's chill. The young beech was yet to sprout and the leaves were conspicuously missing leaving the whole area vulnerable to wind. It was mere steps to the slightly chopped up area in front of the dog kennel and as soon as she got close all of the dogs barked. Jackeran started it, questioning who was outside but they fell silent when they detected the comforting and recognizable scent of their owner. Jackeran thought about it but he knew what was going on. He stood on his back legs, his front legs high up the metal dog cage inside the door but it was futile, he couldn't see out of the front of the kennel, he could only imagine what was happening.

He heard his mistress go to the shed. He heard the door open. He heard the tin open and he sensed the movement of magic as she picked up the record.

Angel carried the record back to the house. She was careful and bemused as she went back into the main house and locked the door behind her.

Widget put a hand up to stop Wizel as he leant so far forwards from their hiding place that he nearly fell out into the room. He stepped back with a slight sound on the stone floor.

The woman walked slowly across the room. Half of the room was on the same level as the front door. The other half was raised slightly. The lower level was next to the kitchen diner, the higher level led to the guest room and had been put in to allow wheelchair access from the guest room which at the time had been the owner's room when she needed it. On the upper level there was a long old fashioned 1970s style stereo gram which was a long wooden piece of furniture.

She lifted the lid and turned the "on" knob. The machine leapt into life. The light came on for the radio and Radio One filled the concentrated silence.

There was a loud electronic thunk as it turned on. There as a crackle as the power ran through it. The room was illuminated by it as 78 was selected by moving the black plastic bar on the record deck and 33rpm. The record slipped onto the central bar and sat on the stack bar. A quick pinch with a finger and it slipped down over the bar and landed gently on the turntable. Another flip of a switch and the turntable started to rotate.

Widget was holding what would have been a breath if she could actually breathe. The woman was also. Wizel was facing the other way with his hands over his head waiting for something dramatic and possibly dangerous to happen.

The turntable revolved as the arm of the stereogram picked up, the arm swung across to the record and gently settled the needle into the groove.

Music filled the air, the room and the world. A Weaver of Dreams by Nat King Cole.

Widget felt the magic as did Wizel. A tear rolled down Wizel's face. He really wanted to step out into the room and share the moment. He was so tempted but he knew that he shouldn't be seen by any mortal. They weren't ready to see what was really out there yet. It did make him feel lonely though.

In a cave in North Wales, under Dynas Emrys, something stirred. Something woke up.

In a cavern a woman lay on a table in a glass coffin. The coffin was surrounded by eternally living red roses which grew out of the stonework around the cave. Her face was young, though that was unrealistic for the years she had existed. Her lips were as red as the roses. Her pale skin reflected light from the ever burning candles that had been set around her coffin. Her deep red dress was plain with lacing up the bodice and hand embroidered lace decoration around the neck. It was meticulously laid out with each fold neatly placed. Her eyes were shut until the sound of the music filled the cavern.

She opened her eyes and reached up and pushed the lid off of the coffin.

It was hinged and opened easily.

She sat up and looked around the room, her eyes blinking as the candles filled the darkness that she had felt for so many years with light that made her eyes sting. She pulled herself up. Her muscles lazy from little use. She got to her feet, wobbling slightly, and stepped over the side of the coffin and jumped down onto the dusty floor. Her tiny red satin ballet shoes becoming instantly covered in dust.

Sleepily she stretched her long white arms, her

fingers reaching into the air and she rubbed her eyes. Music filled the air and she had to listen. It filled her very soul and reminded her of who she had been before her enforced long, long sleep.

She took a step forwards, staggering slightly as her legs were weak from her long sleep. Then she remembered it all. The thoughts and memories bursting through her sleep soaked mind. She was the Weaver of Dreams. That was her job, her life and all that she had been, was and ever would be and she had been denied this for far too long. She sighed, holding her hands together in a silent prayer and vow that it would never happen again.

She whispered even though she knew there was nobody there to overhear and silence her. "I am the Weaver of Dreams. I call on my dream mares and stallions. Come and take dreams to those who need them. Nightmares, come and take dreams to those who need to know the fear of the night and the dark things in life. Come my children, we have work to do."

Silence, a moment when she wondered if things had changed so much while she slumbered in the arms of Morpheus. Were they all trapped as she had been? Were they dead, killed by mankind's neutrality or despair? A cold chill ran through her and in panic she looked around the confines of her cave which had been her prison for so many years. What if? The thought gnawed at her. There was nothing she could hold onto. Her faith and hope were leaves on the wind now that she had been trapped for so many years. Her confident complacency of the previous time evaporated into the ether. Was she standing alone in a cave beneath the ancient place where once Dragon Kings had met or was this the beginning of the return of dreams where her dream horses would gallop majestically to answer her call? Her self doubt was debilitating, it was silencing her call and drowning out her inner voice with a cacophony of other unwanted voices. She knew that to do anything her call must be pure, her intent definite and the sound would then vibrate through the ether can call them, if they were indeed still there.

She calmed herself. Instinctively she visualized herself as a tree, her roots growing down into the earth. The red energy of Mother Earth flowed like a river up through her filling her from her feet to her head. The doubt faded away as the red energy cleansed her and her voice sounded like a bell, calling the dream horses from their rest, from their prisons, from all the places that the darkness had sought to hide or imprison them.

Her call was answered by a thunderous sound of hooves even though the mares would have no solid hoof to hit a solid ground to make such a noise.

Horses appeared everywhere. They came through the walls, leaping down from heights and through the ceiling and the floor. Manes and tails flowed free in the non existent wind. They came to stand in lines then as one their reared up and let out a neigh that echoed through the ether. Some were emaciated, some bore scars, some bore deep cuts where they had been bound. Their manes lacked luster and their coats were patchy from years of entrapment by the Goblians. Every horse on Planet Earth heard their cry of freedom and answered and many horse owners were left wondering what had happened.

Woken from their slumber many horse owners ran to their horses' aid only to find their horses calm and content. Social media hummed with the discussions and questions but despite a myriad of theories nobody knew why but they wrote it in their diaries and it was recorded for all time.

A white mare stood before the Weaver of Dreams. Her body and stance the mirror of the white Lipizzaner horses of the Spanish Riding School of Vienna. The Weaver had always thought that. The black Nightmares the mirror of the glorious black Friesian horses. It had always bemused her that the black Nightmares had long flowing feathers around their hooves, the white Dreammares having none.

The white mare bowed her head and then shook it.

The horses waited, stallion and mare standing shoulder to shoulder so that they could fit in the cave. Some were not quite inside as there was no room for them despite the cave being at least a hundred feet long. They stood half in the cave, half in the wall. As one their backs sprouted feathered wings, their hooves sprouting smaller wings as they stamped and pranced in an equine tattoo before they stood silent, waiting, wings furled awaiting their Mistresses' command. Injuries healed, scars faded and bodies filled out until they stood, as one, majestic and glorious.

The Weaver smiled as elation flowed through every sinew of her body. She looked down the lines of majestic horses who towered above her and couldn't help being slightly daunted by them. "My friends, I have been asleep a long time. I am sure you all have had experiences, good or bad which are tales to be told and which should be told. Take your time to be who you are again. The problem is that I can't remember what to do?" She really couldn't. She reached into her memory but she couldn't remember how to make dreams. She had been asleep in a void of nothingness, steeped in the mundanity of the mortal world, for too long.

The head mare bowed down so that her nose was level with the Weaver, she reached forwards and put her head over the Weaver's shoulder. All was silence, all the Weaver could hear was the drip, drop of water on its eternal journey from the surface to the underground aquifer which flowed to the sea. In her head the Weaver heard a voice. "You will remember."

The Weaver looked around the cavern. It was bare other than the horses and the coffin that had been her prison. Then she spotted something. There was an alcove in the far wall, a small one and in the alcove there was a wooden goblet bound with metal. It looked old, very old and as she noticed it she could feel the power coming from it.

The Dream Weaver walked towards it. Her legs were weak and she almost fell as the horses parted to make a path for her. The head mare stepped beside her so that the Weaver could hold her mane to walk, aided by the mare's solid frame, to the alcove.

She climbed up onto the rocks in front of the alcove and reached up. Her fingers could barely touch it. But, by climbing on the mare's back she was able to reach it and she lifted it from its rest and climbed down. There was nothing in it. She had expected something inside or something to happen but nothing did.

The horses parted and the dripping water began to coalesce into a rivulet and the rivulet increased into a stream which flowed across the floor of the cavern, growing deeper and deeper.

Some of the horses were startled by this and backed away but, after recovering their composure, they managed to fall back into line, leaving what was now a deep stream flowing across the cave.

The Weaver thought about it. "Well I suppose I should put the water into the goblet."

The water was cave chilled icy cold. It sparkled as the fresh spring water filled the goblet and it seemed to glow. It was then that the Weaver thought about how she was managing to see anything at all in the cave which should have been dark. It enticed her and she knew what the right thing to do was. She took a deep breath and then took a long drink from the goblet. The chilled water ran over her tongue, filling her mouth and she swallowed it.

Then she remembered.

She opened her hand and touched each of the horses as they came to her, one by one, before galloping off through the walls. Through the morning they galloped which was night for some, finding all those who were still asleep. The rest circled the world, waiting for night to fall and for the rest to go to sleep.

That night everyone dreamed. The night air was full of it and by the morning creativity flowed as the dreams were written about, spoken about and thoughts turned to what all the dreams meant.

2 ALL ABOARD THE GHOST TRAIN

Written by Stellastar Widget, the Frixian

Why does time go so slowly when you want it to go fast and fast when you want it to go slowly?

Today we wanted it to go fast so that we can get out on our trip. I couldn't believe it when I found out we were booked to go. The tickets were bought ages ago and I have kept them safe in my basket. Gadget has checked them so many times today to make sure they aren't lost. Now they are safely packed in Angel's handbag and we are nearly ready to go. But we still have to wait. My basket is waiting on the table and very soon we will get in there so that we are easy to carry. We wouldn't want to get lost as we have to drive into town and get on the steam train. That may not be so easy as Angel and her friends have to, or shall I say are doing because they want to, go in costume. Long dresses, umbrellas and carrying us as well could prove a problem and we certainly don't want to get wet.

I love my dress. It is long and purple. I also have a lovely sparkly tiara as well. It did try on a demon mask but that didn't fit and it made my ears itch.

I tried on a lot of costume which was fun.

The week has been really dull for us this week. Someone tried to steal our pony friends but they were caught. Angel now has someone to keep her happy and he was great when there was trouble. But, to be careful all the sheds are now locked so we can't get the goats out to play with them at night. What do we do when it gets dark now and everyone has gone to bed. Our nightly rides are a thing of the past.

To cheer us up Angel and Niall are taking us on the Vale of Rheidol Railway. We are going on a Ghost Train and it is really exciting. Have I said that already, sorry. Now, pardon my ignorance but if it is a Ghost Train would we have to be dead and ghosts to go on it? How can a Ghost Train work? Surely the passengers, being dead, wouldn't be able to pay for a ticket?

I looked it up on the internet and now it makes sense. The steam train runs every day on certain days in the summer and specifically now for Halloween and at

Christmas. It is a lovely old train with carriages, just the covered ones this time of the year. The staff will be decorating it and it must be wonderfully atmospheric. Spiders and ghoulish and other fun things.

How can a day take so long? Then I have everything ready and it really isn't fair that the band can't come too. They would love it but they are relying on us to tell them all about it afterwards.

The Vale of Rheidol Railway is very old. Not as old as us of course. It was authorised by an Act of Parliament on the 6th August 1897. Back then it would have been modern. It was what is known as a narrow gauge railway which is ideal for passing through difficult terrain. This is what it was built for.

The animals are all fed, watered and put to bed. Tick, tock the racing clock and now it is time to be going and we have to make sure we have everything. Time is of the essence, I love that comment. Time is now not on our side as we have to get to the train before it starts and everyone has to have their costume, makeup and wigs in place.

Hair brushed, make up on, costume in place and we all ran to the car through the rain. We were a little late.

When everyone was ready with their seat belts on the

car streaked through the darkness. Green leaves, trees and fields flashing past. I knew they were out there but it was dark so I just had to imagine them out there. I hadn't been in the car driving into town before you see.

White fluffy sheep looked up lazily and contemplated us with a combination of curiosity and boredom once they realized we weren't going to hurt them.

The road streaked out in front of us, captured in the headlights. Nobody was about. It was as if the whole world had been abducted by aliens. Who would know?

Lights were on in houses but who knows if anyone was home. What if a Zombie Apocalypse had happened and we had missed it? It can be like that sometimes when you drive in the countryside. There are rarely people walking in the roads and lights will be on in houses where people are enjoying themselves with their televisions and other media. The road rolled on but still there were no people. Were they all on the railway and were we the last to go? Drive Sarah, drive carefully but drive.

Sarah is Frixian Friend. She came from England to spend Halloween with us and she is coming on the Ghost Train too. She is going to be looking after Gadget to make sure she doesn't get into any mischief.

Aberystwyth got closer and closer and the time ticked on. Then we were there, we pulled into the car park and everyone was ready to go as the rain fell and bounced off of the windscreen. We had four minutes to spare so the train wouldn't go without us now. We weren't there yet. We had to get out of the car and get to the train yet. That it was raining didn't help. What a juggling act to carry everything. Costume, cloaks, high heels and wet pavements didn't make life any easier.

We didn't run, we walked as we had a minute to go before the train left. We were nearly last so even though we were on the platform we had to walk quite a way along the train before we found a carriage with any empty seats in it.

Families sat together with sweets and children in costume with smiling happy faces. They looked out of the windows at us. Parents smiled happily, content that their children were being amused. They had bags of sweets. I could smell them and almost taste them. A joyous time of spooky fun. I love spooky fun. It is my favourite time of the year. Creatures like me can come out to play. Then I am a puppet so I suppose as long as I don't move and let Angel do all the work everything would actually be alright anyway.

I couldn't see too much, just a few faces where doors were open but those carriages were full. We walked up and down the little carriages in the rain. The train looked great too. Cobwebs hung in the windows, black lace curtains hid the people inside making it look really dark inside. Although of course it wasn't.

There were lots of people and every carriage was packed out. We did find somewhere but we couldn't sit together.

It was dark, both inside and outside the carriage. Then someone put on an iPad and bang went the atmosphere. It was light and no longer scary.

Someone had worked really hard on decorating the carriage. It was festooned with skeletons, masks and cobwebs. Material and lace was draped across the windows like curtains. It looked amazing.

This was Halloween after all and all manner of nasty creatures are wandering about unseen by the mortal world. I can see them though and feel them. They are out there. All I hope is that this train keeps going when we are further up the valley as a train full of caged children could be far too tempting a treat for some creatures.

It all looked so innocent. Smiling guards and then they locked us in. Was this a plot? We had happily got into a train and on the window there was tape saying "Enter at your own risk". What about "Elf and Safety". For the good of this Frixian I don't want to get eaten by something bigger than me or attacked by Goblians. I know they are about tonight.

They have been much more active for days. I know they are in the woodlands next to the house and their leader Gishnak was very close to the smallholding the other night, almost to the door. I could smell him. He can't come in as our magic protects the place but he seems to be getting stronger.

Now I can smell him here. A waft of him as the doors were locked.

He could be in the carriage. I can still smell him but the scent of those things does linger so it could be residual. So many people with bags, he could be in any of those bags and the owner wouldn't know. Other Goblians could be here too. With all the masks and costumes a Goblian could be sitting in the carriage dressed up like all the other children.

This is not going to go smoothly. I know that. I can see that Gadget is worried as well. Sarah can't hear what Gadget says but I can. Should I say something?

Too late, the whistle blew somewhere down the platform and the train juddered into movement and pulled out of the station. Angel opened the window and smoke wafted past us into the distance like its own ethereal ghost on its way to the spirit world. Six minutes past six, I could see Angel's watch.

Is that relevant or an omen?

We are on our way to Devil's Bridge and we are in a locked carriage, only openable from the outside and there is nothing I can do to warn everyone that there are Goblians about.

The train rumbled along the tracks. The rhythmical sound and the gentle swaying of the carriage lulling us into a false sense of security.

The smell of the smoke was so different to anything I had smelt before. The excited babble of chatter as children talked to each other and their parents reminded me that this was supposed to be fun. But is it? Am I just a worrier? Perhaps.

The train pulled out of the station and through Aberystwyth and as it passed along the lights of buildings passed by the window. Tiny fireflies of light in the velvety darkness reminding me that there was life out there. Car headlights and other lights reflected on the rain soaked road as we crossed the level crossing and cars had to wait for us. The train rumbled on and we were thrown into darkness as we left the town.

Oh well, too late to worry about it all now. We are

on our way. I do however feel like a snack in a box being driven past monsters. Out there in the dark things were lurking. They were behind every tree, the normal ethereal creatures there as well but many of them were hiding and I don't blame them.

The veils were thin tonight, the ghosties and ghoulies and long legged beasties ruled this night and even they were trying to avoid the things that go bump in the night. Ethereal things and things more solid were fighting each other, preying on each other. It is a war out there. The ghosts wafted around, wandering their way, some lost, some with purpose. It was obvious that they didn't like the ghouls. They stepped out of their way to avoid them. The dirty cadaverous bodies of the ghouls were perhaps in their consciousness an inelegant memory of the bodies that they had once had. The long legged beasties were lurking in dark corners. There, by a tree, a leg hanging down. For a moment before the creature climbed up into the tree out of sight.

A fox ran through the undergrowth. The beast moved like lightning and reached down, grabbing the hapless creature and raising it up into the tree.

It squealed and its life was gone.

This lovely old carriage creeping slowly into the night past dark hallows and ancient trees. Creatures were everywhere and I could see them but sadly those in the carriage couldn't, they are human and humans can't see these things unless the creature wants them to.

Out in the darkness an Ent, a tree spirit, waved its branches at the train, waving a warning? It was a kind thought but to anyone else on the train it would just look like a tree waving in the wind. The Ent's Dryad peeked around his ancient trunk and looked around. Only fleetingly. Her pale green hair glowed in the darkness, illuminated by the ethereal light of the magic which shrouded everything and allowed such creatures access to the mortal world. This was new. I had seen other Halloweens. There was much more power out there this year and many, many more creatures. If it had been daylight then her hair would have reflected all the colours of nature. Night made it duller. He diaphanous gown was concealed by the darkness but I had seen their dresses before and they were magnificent in their simplicity. As she saw me she blew me a kiss, her blessing of hope I hope and perhaps she gave us a thought for a moment and hoped that we would survive.

Further down the track I saw a misty light amongst the electrical glow coming from buildings we were passing. A White Lady was wandering along the tracks. That is never a good portent. She is a harbinger of trouble to come. Her tall elven features were hidden in the dark but from her silhouette I know what she is and it sent a shiver down my spine. Alright down my spiritual spine as the puppet of course feels nothing.

The train rumbled on and I began to relax and enjoy watching the creatures at their nightly wanders as the train passed them. Many were oblivious to everything around them. Some stopped to look at the train. That was creepy.

The train juddered to a stop. The drapes still swinging before falling still. Now I'm worried. This is terrible as we are stuck in the darkness with all those creatures around us. Anything could happen. Goblians are out there. Their scent filled my senses and it was much more than the residual smell in the carriage. It could be anywhere or there could be more than one. The good thing is that Goblians' eyesight is not great. They spend most of their life lurking in the dark so sight is not the best of their senses. On the Ghost Train there was noise, lots of it. This is what attracts them and this is very dangerous. We are not safe at all.

Thankfully the train moved off again and rumbled along the track. On and on into the darkness. Then we stopped again and a loud explosion rang out, silencing the children in the carriage. Another and another. Movement outside, people in costume with masks on running down the side of the train knocking on the windows. Faces appeared at the window and the carriage was filled by ghoulish screams of excited children. They knew too that these were people from the Railway and not some other dangerous creature.

The window was open, that was probably a mistake. Just as I thought that a ghoulish hand reached through the window and tried to grab me. Fingers reached towards me and thankfully Angel was watching and I felt myself whisked away as the hand grabbed empty air. The strong arms that would have dragged me out of the train to certain death pulled back and for a moment it was quiet.

Screams rang out as passengers were attacked. This is what the sound of death must sound like. People screaming and dying or having fun? It was hard to tell. I couldn't see them, only those in my carriage and they were enjoying the fake fear, the safe fear like rollercoaster fear. Then again there have been a couple of instances where that fear wasn't so safe either.

On a night like this who would know if the real monsters had already killed the railway workers and taken their place. The driver was in an open engine, what if he was dead? Then again, this is an official tour, surely we are safe?

More explosions, fireworks of course but in the darkness and with the screaming they felt very real.

I've been through so many wars before I came here. So many times when those sounds were real. In fact, it is a bit of a travesty that in such a terrifying world children seek thrills of being attacked and having explosions set off for their amusement. It made me smile in a way, it was a bit of innocence.

The children screamed but they were very brave. Rather than running away from the window and hiding they were climbing on chairs to get close to the window and discussing what superpowers they could have to defend themselves. One wanted punching and a cold chill ran through me. What if he punched the next monster who reached through the window and that being a railway worker or volunteer that would not be a good situation. As they laughed and screamed they were having a great time. It was a Ghost Train after all but they had no idea of the danger they were really in.

Goblians, the smell was strong. They were everywhere and I feared for the volunteers outside as well.

More explosions as I looked out of the window helplessly, just hoping that we would move off soon. Then it went spookily silent and the train moved on.

I looked over at Gadget, she too was worried so we used our magic and stepped out of our cloth puppet bodies. We couldn't do much as puppets but in our

Frixian Spirit manifestations we could at least have a look around and of course effect the Goblians.

I raised up from the little cloth puppet, my white ethereal body adorned by a diaphanous gown somewhat like that worn by the Dryad but white.

Gadget did as well and together we walked through the carriage, through chairs, people and the walls as they were not solid to us.

There was at least one Goblian in each carriage. They saw us but they kept in their hiding places. They were weak as they were newly into the world but by midnight they would have their full power. They were weak because the children were happy, they feed on despair and there was little of that around. They wouldn't challenge us in their ones and twos but there were more out there and together they could be a problem.

Something had to be done but attacking them one by one could harm the children as it would involve throwing magic around and that can mean collateral damage.

Now I wonder. Goblians have a weakness, popping candy. As there are sweets everywhere there could be some on board the train. All we have to do is find it.

Outside I could smell and see the Goblians getting closer. They were targeting the train and I don't think it was because we are here. That many children in one place who are not going to run away, it was perfect.

Please let there be candy on board. We began to run, carriage after carriage and then in the last carriage we were in luck. There was a bag of it in a carrier bag of other sweets. Now of course we had the problem that we were both in Frixian Form so we couldn't touch the mortal world. The puppets were right down the other end of the train and we couldn't get them through the doors or walls. So close! I needed hands to open that packet.

Or I needed someone to do it for me.

I stepped off of the train. The Goblians were about fifty yards away and they didn't seem to have seen me. So, I walked to a tree and touched it. A dryad stepped out of it. She looked nervous but she tried a smile.

Her voice was silvery. "Frixian, why do you call me from my tree on this dangerous night?"

"Creature of the Woods I need your help. There are Goblians in the woods and they are attacking the train. I need your help to open a packet of popping candy so that I can lure them away from the children."

The smile dropped from her face. "Why should I help children? They come to our woods and damage the trees. They climb into our branches and they leave their rubbish at our feet. Why should I?"

She turned to go but I reached out and grabbed her arm. It was an instant reaction and probably the wrong one but all I could think of doing. She hesitated and looked down at my hand then glared at me and her look was truly terrifying.

She hissed. "Unhand me alien creature if you want to live. I will not help you."

A deep voice boomed from within the tree. "If the Goblians are powerful in our woods we will lose more than a few children can achieve. Help her or you will find another tree tonight."

Now the Dryad was really angry but she hesitated and I let her arm go. "Very well. I will help you but I ask something in return. In the future you will be in a place which is ancient and will have ancient woodland. I ask that you protect the ents and dryads there."

I nodded. It was hardly a difficult task as I'd do that anyway.

All three of us floated back to the train. The Goblians

had formed up into a line and they stood there, slavering in anticipation. They were waiting as they knew that the longer the train stood still with nothing happening the sooner boredom would set in and the children would become awkward. That would fuel them enough to make them powerful enough to control everyone on the train.

The dryad reached into the bag, took the packet of popping candy out as she could touch the paper wrapper even though she was ethereal.

In the confusion the occupants of the carriage didn't see the packet float out of the bag and out of the window. They didn't see it float down the train onto the tracks. They didn't see the top of the packet ripped off and the contents poured onto the tracks.

Her task done the Dryad disappeared, leaving us standing beside the popping candy and as we looked back the Goblians were underneath the train. Sinuous fingers reaching up and soaking in the children's angst and the parents' frustration and they were becoming powerful.

Long green noses sniffed out the candy treat. Clawed feet flapped onto the gravel as they edged forwards, loathed to leave the empowering area around the train.

Then as one they could not resist the smell of the

candy and they charged, each wanting to get there first and get the most of the delicious treat.

The timing was perfect as the train started to move. The Goblians were advancing fast and we only just managed to float up over them and return to the puppets on the train as the train began to gather speed. Then it began to judder slightly as it bumped over the Goblians, flattening them and killing any who fell under the wheels. They were too intent on the candy and it was easy to imagine them being flattened, the others oblivious as they fought each other to be able to eat the sweets.

As the train moved off the children were happy again and the Goblians lost their power source. As they began to fade the train claimed them, as did other creatures who had been alerted by the gathering of so much power in one place. Creatures of the night capitalised on the Goblians' misfortune and attacked, shuffling and snuffling from the shadows to eat their fill and take their revenge on the sniveling creatures.

The train rumbled on and pulled into Devil's Bridge Station. The name on the sign was ominous but the welcome was warm. Pumpkins had been carved, candles lit and decorations had been carefully placed to make the place look festive.

There was a coffin at the end of the platform. Time to relax. All the happiness and fun here would keep the Goblians far, far away. The lights were lit and the pumpkins flickered their mock horrific smiles to entertain the arriving guests. They were so brave those children all, there was no pride to come before a fall. With happy face who cares about the rain. It might just wet us as we alight from the train.

Happy people climbed down from the train and filled the platform. Moving as one along the platform towards the large marquee that had been set up for the meal. Empty stomachs soon to be filled as the music did play. Along the platform we all did walk, for a piggy roast that would need no fork.

Fear behind us, the scares are gone, food and light now and a brighter song. The Monster Mash is a cheerful tune, spiders, cobwebs and creatures of the moon.

As everyone got of the train it was a time to see just how many people had been on that train and how popular the trip was. No wonder they said book early and I am glad that Angel did. They came from everywhere, emerging from dark carriages to join the crowd moving along the platform towards the station restaurant.

The crowd was big and moved so slow. They rain did fall but it was a glorious show. The rain did fall on one and all, and poor Sarah only had a shawl.

The marquee and building had been decorated for the party. Music rang out and all the happiness of the play horror of Halloween surrounded us.

I can't help remembering the old ways though, the time when this night was one of revered honour to the loved dead. The night before All Hallows, all holy. A time for leaving candles for the loved ones who may come back to visit in the darkness and need a light to bring them home. How this ended up with children knocking on doors to terrify old people into giving them sweets I do not know. But, like many old ways it is at least remembered albeit in an altered and much different form.

There was almost a queue for tables there were so many people there. Sarah found a table and sat there to keep it for us and I was unceremonially dumped in my basket. I would love to look around but I can understand. Angel can't eat a bun and drink her drink and keep me looking around as a puppet and we are safer in our basket.

Angel was right, there were too many children with apple sauce soaked sticky fingers about and my cloth body doesn't wash.

In the darkness of the basket I have to think. We have the journey back yet. It would be easier if it was a safe journey. No doubt the children would be tired and that is a powder keg of them being tetchy and bad tempered. That would feed the Goblians so making them sleep would be a good idea or at least to calm them down. Also, we had just caused an unknown number of Goblians to be killed so no doubt their colleagues would not be happy and would likely attack us on the way back if they can. I have to make sure that they can't. There were hundreds of them out there and they aren't going to be happy as they haven't managed to harm the children or feed off of them.

I did the Mash, I did the Monster Mash, yep, we did and we used a train. The music ran out over the happy gathering and I was quite enjoying it from the basket. The lull before the storm I suppose. There is something happy about Halloween and I suppose other countries see things differently. The Day of the Dead and such like. People love to dress up and the train tonight makes it so much more special.

The meal will be done soon so I had better create a spell to protect everyone on the way home. Energy is there, the happiness I can use and using that energy will make the children tired which is a double result. So I'll cast the spell.

As we left the station and stepped back onto the platform it was a chance to see the train engine. It was magnificent big and old. The carriages were wood but the train was metal. I hadn't seen it before when we arrived but now was a chance. It was a mountain train, not designed for long journeys.

It is getting late now and the children are slowing down, their batteries spent. They are still excited but much more subdued, the spell must be beginning to work, coupled with their natural exhaustion. Enthusiasm is drifting into quiet enjoyment and I think the parents are grateful for that. They are tired too and the spell will push that tiredness into sleep. Once the carriage starts rocking that should do the trick.

The seats weren't booked so it is first come first served when it comes to getting back onto the train. The train is also less empty so I am wondering if some people parked their cars up at Devil's Bridge and didn't do the journey back. It makes sense if the children are tired as it is only going to be a run back no doubt and in the darkness it is impossible to see anything out of the window.

The carriage was partly empty and my friends are tired too. They will be asleep too soon. Then hopefully we'll just rock our way gently back to Aberystwyth.

Thinking about it, on the way out I heard someone mention a Haunted Castle. There isn't a castle. Children have such an imagination but on a night like this anything is possible. Merely thinking about a

Haunted Castle, saying it to someone else who thinks about it can bring that castle into being. Such is the way when the building blocks of the world at the smallest level are a bit random.

Everyone else is now asleep but we won't. We have to keep watch. It is dark so I can't really see who else is in the carriage. It definitely isn't full.

Hopefully we will be alright now.

Hold on, the train just stopped. Why would it stop on the way back when it is obvious there is no more entertainment? Great, a blue light out there in the darkness. That definitely shouldn't be there. Heads up Gadget, I think we have trouble.

It is in the trees and it is getting closer. It could be good or bad but as it is Halloween I think I'll assume the latter. It is hovering and dancing, almost willing me to get of the train and follow it. The veils are thin. Anything could be out there.

It was then that in what would have been the silence I noticed the quiet music and eerie noises which had been pre-recorded for the trip back. Or perhaps the way there but had gone unnoticed because of all the other noise. That wasn't anything to worry about. The plastic skeleton that was hanging on the wall was. It had been looking the other way when I last looked. There, it moved again, looking down the carriage instead of the other way. Thankfully as it was attached to the carriage by its head there isn't much it can do. Its arms and legs moving are unnerving but as long as the string holds it is not a problem. That it is moving at all is a problem.

There is something going on and it won't solve itself so it is time to leave my basket and go and see what I can do. There is no point going in Frixian Spirit, I think I may need to be a bit more solid for this one.

The first thing to do is to check out what I can see outside. The blue light is still moving around. On the other side there is a green one. In themselves they are not dangerous but I don't know what they are, we are stopped and that together could be a problem. And the large castle with pointed turrets that is now outside the window definitely wasn't there earlier, last week or last year.

The train obviously isn't going to move on and the doors are locked. That should keep the people on the train safe. The windows aren't locked so I suppose my first task should be to make sure that they all are. Great, out in the rain, slippery train side and a cloth body. This is not going to be pleasant.

Gadget isn't keen on this either but there is nothing for it, we have to do it.

The window was heavy when you only have a cloth

body and determination. Magic does help and eventually we pulled the glass window down. I was right about the train side as well. The painted wood was wet and if I jump down onto the ground I'd never get back up to the window. I'd have to make my way along the slippery walls and then climb from carriage to carriage.

Gadget smiled. "Magic it. You can close the windows with magic."

I can you know. It isn't an easy spell but by combining two I could do that and with the option of getting very wet the only other alternative I think I should.

Right, that is the windows closed and magically locked. Now we have to see what is going on with that castle.

"Gadget, I can't see anything out there, it is pitch black. Just the glow from the castle. Did we bring torches?"

Gadget sighed. "Yes but they are in the car for when we get back. We didn't bring them with us in the basket. Shall we try to get the train moving again? We could see what is happening with the engine and the driver. It is a long way down though, and very wet."

Widget looked out into the darkness, her long black curls blowing in the wind. "That seems like the best idea. If we get down we'll have to get back up again though."

Gadget was already pulling belts off of the costumes of theh sleeping travelers and tied each one together and to the door handle before throwing the rest of it out of the window so that the could easily climb down and back up again.

They climbed down onto the wet gravel which ran along the side of the rails and in the darkness they could smell Goblians. They ran fast, very fast for two little cloth puppets. No human could have been able to see them move and they got to the engine.

As they climbed up onto it carefully and peeped over to look into the main cab they saw there was someone there, someone who looked like they shouldn't be. There was a tall figure in a black cloak which reached to the ground. The hood was pulled up so they couldn't see its face until it turned around. The green glowing eyes were an indication that it wasn't the driver so they both hid. Like two torches the eyes illuminated everything in their path which included the two Frixians who were trying to hide but were not quick enough.

The skull face was illuminated by the eyes, its skeletal hands reached out towards the pair of

Frixians who leapt back before the bony fingers could get a grip on them. Widget landed on Gadget who squealed before they both scampered into the black and soggy undergrowth. There were enough bushes there and they crouched down behind one, cowering close to the damp loamy soil.

The skeleton's eyes illuminated the area like a searchlight. They were outside the glow from the train carriages and in the darkness behind the bush so the skeleton couldn't see them however hard it looked. The green glow of the castle behind them threatened to reveal them but they knew about it so they kept very still.

The scent of Goblians was joined by something dead.

Gadget tugged Widget's sleeve. "Shall we go and see if there is an answer in the castle? I know, the last place we want to go but there is no coincidence here."

"I agree. We need to find the driver or that train isn't going anywhere."

They ran very fast and like a flash they were at the castle. For good or bad they stood in front of the large wooden castle doors. The wood planks were covered in cobwebs as was the arch that swept above them. Nobody had been there in a very long time. There was a huge door knocker but the two little

Frixians were in no hurry to knock and have the door answered if they could avoid it and sneak in some other way. They knew there would be no welcome there.

The window to the right was cracked so Widget carefully lifted out a piece of glass big enough for her to climb inside. That was something she had to do very carefully as she really didn't want to tear herself.

Inside the castle the room the other side of the window was a huge open hall. Along the middle was a large table which was set out for dinner and almost groaning under the weight of many tasty treats and other food. Sweets and all manner of sugary confectionary in the brightest of colours was laid out. Fatty treats and all manner of the tasty but not good for you things that parents usually rationed to their children were laid out ready for eating. It was a feast set out for children and it was then that Widget realised that she could see it because the lights had come on.

The lights were bright and shiny and the music that had also started up was spooky but happy like it had been at Devil's Bridge.

Gadget had also climbed inside.

Widget smiled. "It is too obviously a trap for

children. I don't need to tell you to touch nothing. No good can come from here. This is a Haunted Castle and no doubt we'll be meeting the Haunts soon enough."

They walked past the oh so tempting table without a further thought for it. Their concentration was on the rest of the room and finding an exit. There was one in the form of a big black definitely not welcoming door which was at the back of the hall behind the table. I was open a crack which made it all the more unwelcoming as that was too much of an invitation to be a good thing.

There didn't seem to be any other option so they opened the door and slipped through it into a room filled with coffins with their lids off.

Widget smiled. "Oh well, Haunted Castle, room full of coffins, here we go."

The room was dusty and cobweb filled as if nobody had been there for a while but they knew that someone must have been. It was an odd thought for two Frixians standing in a room full of coffins as the bodies in them sat up all as one but Widget couldn't help wondering if there was a spell or can of spray which put all the dust and cobwebs in place.

The bodies were beginning to stand up but rather than run away Widget looked around the room as

Gadget grabbed hold of the door behind them to make sure it didn't shut by itself.

The room seemed to be empty but in the gloom at the back of it there could just be seen a table and on the table was a shovel. Widget's mind was racing, shovel, coal, train, it had to be important. So she knew she had to get it, even though the bodies in various stages of decomposure were by now almost climbing out of the coffins. Widget took a deep breath and faster than a speeding bullet she covered the distance to the back of the room, grabbed the shovel and as she ran back she walloped each of the teetering bodies back into their coffins. They immediately started to try to climb out again but by then Widget was the other side of the room.

Out of the room they ran as there were no other doors in there.

Gadget caught Widget's arm as they ran into the hall. "We have to find the driver and if someone shovels the coal there must be someone else as well. We need another door. Think hard, if this is a thoughtform castle then if we think hard enough we may well find a door now. This is a Haunted Castle so there is no way we are going to be alone. The bodies in there, just a start."

Widget tried to smile. "That is what I'm worried about. So, where do we start. Those bodies are going to catch up with us if we waste too much time. If this is a castle, which it looks like one and one that would be imagined to look this way then it would have a dungeon wouldn't it? If you are keeping someone against their will then a dungeon would be the place to do it. So we need to get to the dungeon which in most stories and in my imagination would be downstairs somewhere. So we need a downstairs.

Gadget was frantically searching around the room. "We need to find a trap door or something."

Widget noticed the bodies getting closer to the door. "We need to sort that lot out first."

Together they tried to close the door but it was too heavy, either actually or magically heavy. Widget sighed and thought about it. Her Frixian magic swirling around like a mist as the door slammed shut and locked. "Well I hope that the trap door wasn't in there. I'm not even going to think about that. The door must be in here somewhere. Well that dealt with them."

Just as she finished speaking a white figure stepped through the wall. It looked like an old lady wearing a wedding dress. Widget jumped slightly.

"Very Miss Haversham. So, what now?"

The woman's face wrinkled up in a grimace and her

gnarly clawed fingers reached out to try to catch the small puppets as she floated across the room towards them.

Gadget grabbed Widget and they dived under the table. "No you don't Grandma, keep those fingers to yourself."

That was when they realised their mistake as the old woman reached through the table and almost caught them. Her hand touching empty air as the pair of them moved away. As fast as they could the pair were out from under the table and running around the room, far quicker than the faster than human speed that the old lady could manage.

As they ran along the wall they noticed that there was a tapestry and as one they grabbed it and pulled. The tapestry held on for a moment before tipping on its rail and falling aside to reveal the door they had been looking for. They didn't have time to think about it. They opened the door, leapt through and closed it behind them. On doing it they realised immediately that it was a futile gesture when the woman had arrived through a wall but it was better than nothing.

They ran down the corridor beyond and then halted as they realised that it was a corridor full of doors which stretched into the distance. Added to this multiple choice there was also the sound of dragging chains in the distance which was getting closer.

Widget sighed. "How cliché."

Gadget laughed. "Graveyard humour?"

Widget smiled. "Dead right."

The sound of metal on stone was getting closer. The footsteps were all to audible and somewhere there was a scream.

Knowing that the ghost was behind them they ran forwards even though it was towards the chains and footsteps and to their surprise they came to the end of the corridor, a dark archway. The corridor had been lit by torches, there was no light beyond the arch.

As one the two grabbed a torch each although they knew to be careful and were very cautious.

The light and warmth from the torch was in one way reassuring but in another frightening to a puppet made of material. They walked slowly now, afraid of any sparks from the torch until they came to a set of stairs heading down.

Widget smiled. "Down is good. Well down is bad but you know what I mean. Down there we might find the driver and anyone else."

Down they went and the stairs met a spiral staircase and they went down that as well. Down and down.

Until it opened up into a room full of torture equipment which had obviously been used or was in the process of being used. An iron maiden was shut, their torchlight illuminating the slit where they could see that it was occupied. Widget rushed over and opened it up with her magic.

The front of it swung open to reveal a rotting corpse, its eyes still focused in pain and its mouth open in a now silent scream.

The two Frixians leapt back but it didn't move. Similarly the body on the wrack was definitely dead but thankfully from their point of view had been dead for a long time so couldn't have been the driver.

The rest of the room was full of similar equipment which was dirty, rusty and covered in old dried blood.

Only one door out was ominous but there was only one door, it was a created castle so they had already worked out that normal logic would probably not apply. One way to go, no choices, so one way they must go.

They opened it and were rewarded by what were clearly dungeon cells. Five barred cells on either side but of course from the door they couldn't see what was inside. To see they had to go into the corridor.

They stepped forwards until they could see into the first pair of cells. To the right was empty, to the left was empty until they took a step forwards and a little girl appeared in the middle of the room. Her face was in her hands and her blue dress was dirty. Her brown curls were caked in mud and her hair ribbon was untied and hung down one side of her head. She took her hands away and both Widget and Gadget were not wrong when they imagined that there would be something horrific about her face. It was covered in blood and slashed.

Widget looked away and looked back. The room was empty, the girl appeared and she did the same thing again. To Gadget she had stood there all along, crying. "It is an illusion. Are you still seeing her? She isn't real."

Gadget turned around. "We are going to need these." She had pulled down a set of keys from their hook on the wall.

When he heard the voices and saw the light the train driver jumped to his feet and ran to the bars. He'd seen enough strange that he thought nothing of two three foot tall puppets holding torches in the corridor. "I'm over here.

Help us."

The driver and the guard were in cells next to each

other. They were covered in dust and cobwebs where they had been thrown into the cell and both looked tired and fed up. The driver still had his peaked cap in his hand, the other had a face covered in soot. The had was similarly dirty but he clung to it despite all the things that had happened to him.

The lock was low enough that Gadget could put the key in and turn. Wrong key. The next one and the next. Then she dropped the keys as they heard the sound of grating chains in the distance. "What are we going to do? The chains are between us and the way out." She fumbled for the keys and began again. All the keys looked the same in the flickering torch light. Key after key and then the lock gave way with a reassuring click. The door opened and the train driver stepped out into the corridor. He took the keys off of Gadget and began trying the keys on the guard's door while Widget and Gadget guarded the corridor, waiting for something hideous to come into the circle of light generated by the torch.

Widget handed the guard the shovel and all of them started walking back down the corridor.

Widget smiled. "Don't worry about the chains. We heard them on the way in and we didn't meet anything. Now they are behind us. We didn't see anyone on the way in. We can hope it is just a sound. Come on, lets run for it."

They ran and they didn't stop. The ghost hag was in the way at the top of the stairs and Widget ran straight through her. By the time she had recovered her composure they were past her, through the outside door and running back to the train.

They crouched behind the bushes again and watched as the skeleton looked about casually unaware that they were there. In the distance there was a howling and a screaming and it wasn't hard to imagine that the ghouls and ghosts from the castle were on their way to try and recapture their prisoners.

The prisoners didn't want to be recaptured and despite their terror the driver stood up. "That is my train to drive and nobody is going to take it from me." He grabbed the shovel from the guard, ran across the gravel and leapt into the engine.

The skeleton saw him coming and pulled back his hood. Beneath it there was a skull which was expected and the glowing eyes turned towards the driver who hit the skeleton with the shovel. The head came straight off of the skeleton's shoulders and flew into the darkness, the green light extinguished.

The driver then threw the rest off the body off of the train as the guard leapt onto the train and began stoking the engine box with coal.

As he shoveled the creatures from the castle got

closer and they were angry. Some moved faster than others, the corpses shambling, the hag and other creatures floating dangerously fast towards them.

Gadget grabbed coal and started throwing it into the box, so did the driver. They got closer and closer. They were so close that they could almost touch the train as the engine lurched forwards and the train moved off, slowly at first but it soon reached a good speed.

The creatures screamed but as soon as the train moved away they and the castle disappeared leaving no trace.

The train gathered speed and rocked and rolled down the track away from where the castle had been and back to Aberystwyth.

Widget looked worried. "How do we get back to our carriage? We have to get back and sort out the belts before we get into Aberystwyth."

The driver pulled a lever and the train slowed down. "Be quick in case there is anything else out there. Thank you for saving us. I am not sure I believe this but if this isn't a dream then I don't know what else to say."

The train pulled to a halt and Widget and Gadget leapt off of the train, ran along the track and climbed back into the carriage using the belts and then began to untie them. Widget hesitated. "Which belt belongs to which person."

Gadget thought about it. "You know I can't remember. We are going to have to work it out by their costume. We'd better sort the mess out as well.

We're mucky. So is the driver."

Gadget smiled. "Go on, use your magic."

Widget looked down. "I am not sure how much I have left. I've used a lot today. I'll give it a try." She concentrated and the dirt disappeared off of all of them. The belts picked themselves up and floated back to tie themselves back onto their original owners.

As the train juddered forwards Widget and Gadget relaxed and enjoyed the ambiance of the train. The music had started again and the spooky sounds, people slept and in the muted light they were just glad to be alive.

As the train passed over the threshold into Aberystwyth and passed Bookers everyone woke up. They were sleepy and totally oblivious to everything that had happened. Widget and Gadget flopped down to be puppets again and watched as best they could and as best they could replaced themselves where they had originally been put.

The train trundled through Aberystwyth, illuminated by the residual light from the houses either side and pulled into the station and came to a halt.

The passengers gathered their possessions and climbed off of the train oblivious to their adventure.

3 BOULEVARD OF BROKEN DREAMS

Widget's fingers flashed across the keyboard of Angel's laptop. She didn't bother to look up now when someone came in as she knew that she had permission to use it and everyone in the house was a Frixian Friend.

Her words were creeping across the screen.

"It can be very lonely when you are miles from home, whoever you are and wherever home may be.

It has been nearly a hundred years for me now since I was last on my home planet. I still miss the violet skies and gentle breezes which smell of the Zelokis Flower.

My home is a beautiful place. The seasons are similar to those on Earth although the summers are longer and warmer and the winters whiter. There are similarities between my planet and Earth, many, but many differences too. Nature, towns, woodland, mountain and vale. Just different colours. Where Earth has chlorophyll my planet has something similar but it is purple. The main difference is that it is forbidden to live in the wilds. That was decided long ago when settlements first started to grow. Town is town, wild is wild. The only ones allowed to spend time living outside are the herders and the growers and only when they are working. It was a decision everyone voted on and it was a good one. It keeps the wild wild.

Frixians are solid there and we live in tall white towers which are linked by undercover walkways. We have beautiful horse like creatures to travel about with who are friends as much as beasts of burden. The cities are immense in their height as they cannot build beyond their city boundary.

You would probably think that these towers would be difficult to build if that sort of thing interests you. Of course as we have magic it is very easy.

With the wave of a wand, a belief, the right permissions and the right words those stone blocks take the form and shape that we want. Block by block the towers are built. Out younglings like to watch and the architect doing the magic likes to sell tickets. It is great fun as magic shapes the rock into an impenetrable structure so that no weather can blow in and so that the towers stay warm and dry. No draughts make people cold and fire imps keep the towers warm. Each imp is chosen and chooses the family and they tend to stay with that family for life. We know they are happy when they sing, either silently so the family can choose to listen or if they think it is right they will sing to the family and their sound is amazing. They have magnificent voices. Flame Song is one of the most amazing sounds I have ever heard.

In the past it was usual for many of us to come to your planet. This was because of an ancient agreement that we would look after children on the planet while we are needed. We aren't anymore which is sad but now we're needed more than ever.

We hatch from eggs and return to our home to grow up if the eggs hatch anywhere else. We hatched on the TAVERN and were then returned back to our home to grow up. We have to do that to understand who we are, what we are and where we belong. Then we can make our own decisions.

We were hatched by the Android Band mechanics in a hatching box. We went home to grow up and then as soon as we were old enough we returned. We spent our time travelling with the TAVERN which we had part helped to build. We did have a couple of hundred years off a while back to go home again while the TAVERN was commissioned for military use. When it was decommissioned due to the file that handled it being lost the Android Band called us back and we began travelling with the new owners.

That was until someone broke it so that the security protocols were off line. It was part of a plan to steal it. That was when someone killed those owners and stole it and put us in the Cyrogenic Freezing Unit. It was stolen by a couple of thieves. One of them killed the other and tried to sell the technology he had taken from the TAVERN on the planet he had landed on as he didn't know how to fly the ship and the Band weren't going to reveal themselves and tell him. That was his problem and it got him killed too. The equipment in the TAVERN looks like junk when it is taken from the building and away from our magic. He made a deal when they agreed to steal it, then thought he had been cheated and killed his partner in crime. The TAVERN was then left stuck as much of its equipment, though junk, was missing.

The Android Band managed to use a default setting to take the TAVERN to a safe world where it rested for many years. It was ticking over on standby. The safe world was EARTH as it was a protected planet. The TAVERN spent many years hidden on a smallholding in Mid Wales.

To anyone looking it was an old building which decayed and then it became a ruin as the physical stonework fell away and parts of it rotted until it was rebuilt by the smallholding's then owner.

Seasons turned and turned again, years flew by as time marched on. The TAVERN structure was rebuilt as a stable before it was again abandoned. We slept through all this until we were awoken and that is history as they say.

We were awoken to a different world and what we were used to was gone. There are no more Frixians on EARTH now, the Toymaker is gone and life is different.

The magic of the Toymaker was very specific. When a toy is given as a gift The Toymaker gives it his blessing. It is then able to be inhabited by one of our kind. When the toy is given the magic of that gift makes it able to be touched by The Toymaker. The Toymaker used to have a part in making every toy but with mechanisation that ended.

So when you cuddled your bear or doll in the past there would more than likely be a Frixian in it. That cuddle was a thank you to the Frixian for all the sleepless nights the Frixian had keeping the child safe from the Monster in the Wardrobe and the Monster Under the Bed.

Of course only the child knew that the toy was protecting him or her. The toy would remain still when the parent came in and of course the parent had forgotten that they had had a Frixian once too. Some had vague memories of their toys being comforting, some even kept those toys. Some that do still remember were seen as being a little odd.

Now there are too many Goblians around and children are turning away from their toys in favour of computer games. We can't do anything with the games and we can't inhabit a computer, we leave that to Nemesis our friendly AI who is definitely a Frixian Friend. That has left the Goblians free to multiply.

Grannies are no longer knitting toys with love that The Toymaker can turn into a Frixian. Children are no longer keeping their favourite toy that they can cuddle when they are afraid. When the toy is no longer loved it loses its magic and the Frixian must leave. So perhaps there is more of a need to be afraid of the dark now as we are gone and toys are just that now, toys.

We are not unique. We have our friend Quirky who lives with Saffy and Creed who came here to help us with building. They brought their puppet here and Quirky got a new inhabitant. There are other disembodied Frixians we know about and but they do not have puppets to live in. We could only find Quirky one because she was in the TAVERN. Without The Toymaker there is nothing we can do.

There will be others too if we can open the gateways to let the spirits through and find the spirit of The Toymaker to link the spirits to the toys. Perhaps Angel will make some toys for others to inhabit, perhaps she won't. I must talk to her about that. She made a lovely goat a while back, that would do.

The Weaver of Dreams sent me a dream last night. It was an amazing dream that we could bring more Frixians into this world and bring back magic. Of course we have to find out how to do that. It is easy for us to leave, not so easy for us to come back.

I can't help but think that there must be something important nearby. There must be a reason why the TAVERN was brought here as a safe place. Or perhaps we need to take the TAVERN somewhere that there is a gateway or where we can open one. Perhaps we can set up a temporary gateway now until we can find the right place. Finding the right ancient magical place in this world is not going to be easy. It would take ancient magic and a place untouched with the destruction of the mundane world.

On my home world the wizards who aren't naturally magical and who have to learn their craft can create visual magic. They tell the stories and as the words are spoken the images play out in front of the audience. Only the ancient ones can do that. The really experienced wizards who are truly at one with their magic.

Frixian elder magic is different. Our magic is natural and we are born with it. I don't need a wand but it does focus the mind. It isn't the generator or controller of the magic.

The wizards have wands, like any non magical creature. They have amazing wands. They have to make them by themselves and usually make then when they are small children who are first stepping out on their magical journey. It is part of their test to become a wizard. Firstly they have to grow the tree to make the wand. It is grown by magic. Then they have to find the right piece from that tree. Then they have to smooth it using magic. Then they have to enchant it. If they can do all that without the wand then they are capable of great magic when they have it. They learn all that from very old books.

Wizards in my world live in towers like the rest of us but these towers are part of schools. They are always learning and when they have learnt enough they teach. There are many different schools and they don't always get on.

I don't know who teaches the High Magus. That is wizard lore and the rest of us know very little of what goes on in their towers. I would assume he has access to a book that nobody else does and when the old one dies the person who takes over is allowed to see the book.

Each house is associated or I could say serves a coloured dragon. The Dragon houses sponsor a wizard school and if there is ever any fight they will call on that school to assist them. When I say dragons, I mean real scaly lizard like creatures with supreme intelligence and as many political aspirations as the mages do. We Frixians tend to keep well clear of them as they will wind us up in their complications if they can.

There was a time when everyone had a type of magic. They did in your world as well. Our worlds are similar in many ways though our world is of course much more magical. You had magic when you had belief and faith. That was a magical time when you still believed in the magical creatures which inhabit your world. It is odd how you don't believe anymore. The creatures are still there. Then again, looking at a lot of your world it is probably best that they are forgotten and can live in peace.

If you believe something without any possible doubt then that is a big step on the way to making it happen.

When I woke up this morning I smelt something. There was magic in the air, Goblian magic. All I can think is that they must have attacked in the night and their target was our secret magic garden. Our defences are strong enough but that isn't the point. The question is why? It is not direct access to the house and other than a few pretty hanging things and a circle of wooden stump seats there isn't really anything there that would interest them. Or is there?

Now I'm going to have to go out and have a look.

Outside the guest room annex there is a large elderly fuchsia bush. It towers over everyone and it must be very old. Well the original part of the bush is. It puts on new growth every year and is excellent cover for me so that I can sneak about without being seen.

As the leaf cover of summer is gone I will have to be careful. I don't want to be seen by one of the neighbours driving or walking past. They don't come past much but I bet the moment I step outside they will be going somewhere or the other. Then again with so much foliage on the front that doesn't die away I should be alright.

I forget that I am so small and that I can't be seen over the low wall where the fuchsia grows. I'm being over cautious and I really must stop that. Silly me, I forget that humans' eyesight isn't as good as ours and that you don't have magic to feel that something is there.

Widget climbed down from the chair where she had been typing and landed on the floor.

Oscar the golden Jack Russell cross Shui Tsu (Jack Shit) viewed her with interest. He got up from his blanket where he had been sitting beside her, wagged his tail and trotted with her into the guest room.

Widget stroked him. "No my friend, you can't come with me. I need to be secretive."

Oscar looked disappointed but went back to his blanket to wait for her to come back.

The key for the door was where it always was so she took it and unlocked the big glass door. It opened easily, she slipped outside and shut it behind her. She was just in time as Sha're the German Shepherd came bounding into the room to see what was happening. She looked confused and then wandered off to find Oscar who told her all about it.

The leaves had fallen quite deeply and they were damp. That area was rarely cleared as it wasn't used. The brook babbled and tumbled under the bridge that Jeff the handyman had built all those years ago.

The low rumble of the Troll sleeping under the bridge was somehow reassuring. It was impossible to hear with human ears of course but to Widget it was almost deafening as she crossed the bridge.

Humans didn't need to know he was there. He spent almost all of his day sleeping when he wasn't eating. He no longer cooked. His cookpot had been broken many years ago. It rested beside the bridge, full of wild Geraniums. He had broken it when he had vowed never to eat any of the animals in exchange for being able to live in peace in the garden.

It had been a few years ago when the house had first been bought that he lived there and for years he had been able to help himself to the odd sheep or chicken, blaming foxes. When the goats moved in he decided one day that a meal of goat would be a good idea.

So he snuck up the hill one night when it was very, very dark with his big club. He wandered in the shadows up to the shed in the top field and found the door unlocked. His gnarled hand opened the door and he stepped inside. His large feet with big toes felt the soft straw under his feet and his big nostrils spelt the fresh smell of hay.

In the shed two goat kids were sleeping. Their gentle snoring and breathing the only sound in the silence. They were curled up together, nose to tail. One was white, one was black.

He grabbed the black one by the neck and lifted it up, licking his lips. Its stripy face was horrified, its mouth open screaming.

The white kid looked up and there was a sad look on her face. She did not panic, she spoke gently. "Do not kill my half brother. He is all I have left."

The Troll jumped and dropped the baby goat who ran to the other side of the small shed. The white goat looked up at him, her big eyes sad but meeting his look without flinching. He looked down at her. "Goats don't talk."

She looked up at him and her eyes were still sad. "I am a goat but I'm also a fairy friend goat. The fairies come at night and we ride to the stars. As a reward for my service they let me speak to creatures such as you. My sadness brought them to me you see and it was why I was chosen. On the night when my mother died the tear cried by my fairy friend owner fell on a Frixian's head. The Frixian didn't have a body back then, she had only just woken up miles from home herself. The Frixian has looked after us ever since."

Widget smiled as she remembered as she was that Frixian. She had been woken by the primal scream let out by Angel when she had realised that her first goat was going to die despite all she had done. The pure fury and hopelessness of that scream had cut through the dimensions and had woken the Frixian from the cryo unit and activated the TAVERN. That was what had bound the Frixian to her as well and allowed them the telepathic communication.

The Troll looked down at his big club and the sack tucked into his belt.

"I was going to eat your half brother but I won't now."

The little goat looked less worried and less sad. "Thank you, for he is all I have left. My mother is dead, my aunty is dead, my brother is dead and my half sister is dead."

The Troll looked sad. "Why are they dead?"

The little goat shook her white coat. "We got sick and nobody could help us. Only me and my half brother survived. So now we are alone but we have each other. We have our owner as well. She will look after us. She isn't the gentle woman who came from the City anymore. She has grown strong and she would fight you if you harmed us."

The Troll looked sad, remembering when he had lost his mother. "You still miss them?"

Symbel bowed her little head. "I miss my mother. She was wild and stubborn and I didn't know her very long but Eirlys was beautiful to me."

The Troll put his club behind his back as he saw the little one looking at it. A single tear ran from his big eye and down his face. "I won't kill you now little one, or your brother. You are not alone. You will never be alone. You have me as a friend now. I am alone. I have nobody." The little goat snorted as they are want to do. "You are my friend now.

I am Symbel and this is my brother Elrond."

The Troll spent the evening talking to the kids and they parted as good friends. When he went back down the hill he smashed his cook pot and vowed he would never harm another animal himself. However hungry he got he would never again think about killing a goat. He never had to. He lived on the food he shared with the other animals. He boiled the eggs the chickens gave him and he cooked vegetables left for him from the garden. He also discovered he had a real taste for slugs and he made up recipe after recipe. He was loaned books from the house and he made up many recipes of his own. His recipes were so good that he published a book of them in the Troll World called "Slug It to Them". Now many more Trolls eat slugs and are much more welcome to those who know they are there.

The Troll never forgot his little friend and he visited her often as she grew into an adult and had babies of her own. When the wind blew wild he would often go and sit with her and the other goats as more goats arrived just so that they knew that they were safe.

When the wind blew wild he would hold their shed down. There was no other reason why the flimsy shed lasted so long.

He lived under the bridge as that is what Trolls do, beside the magical garden and was happy with is life. He was young when the world was young, he is now old. He preferred to sleep a lot now and dreaming of that magical world we can all get to when we are asleep. That is the problem, he slept too much so evil people got into the garden.

He was snoring as Widget stepped across the bridge. Her toes touched the loamy soil. The green grass clung to the sun soaked patches beneath the trees. The low branches swung around in the gentle breeze. It is a peaceful place, a place of stories, of thought and of magic and contemplation.

Pine needles had built up over generations to create a soft carpet. Ancient fir trees which grew around the edge of it created a wall of green like a tree tower. Plants had to cling to the snickets of light that made their way through their branches. The ancient Yew tree aimed for the heavens, sucking up what light it could. The monkey puzzle tree at the back of the garden was stunted by the lack of light and because someone had trimmed the top off of it but it lived all the same.

In the middle of the clearing Angel had put a ring of

tree chunks to make a storytelling circle. There was a large chair for the storyteller at the head of the circle. It was a gift from a neighbour and one day it will be a magnificent chair when the plants around it grew.

Beside a large tree there was a healing circle. A pile of gemstones and crystals which had been energised by many all over the world in the early days when Angel had been on Facebook, before they changed the settings and made all the groups lose members. Now it rests waiting for others to come and give it the power to heal again. Still sparkling, still waiting.

A sound to the right dragged Widget from her reverie. A putrid smell filled the air and a loud burp silenced the birdsong that Widget hadn't noticed until it was gone. That putrid festering smell of body odour and old socks really didn't fit the beauty of the glade. Smells that the resident troll had long abandoned when he had discovered the magic of soap and the bubbling stream.

Widget turned slowly, scared to find out what she was going to see. She was right to be scared.

There towering under the trees was a very large and very ugly troll and it was not the troll that lived there. He was nearly eight foot of evil, bone gnawing, Frixian eating, foul smelling troll. His warty skin and long pointed nose blocked out the sun.

She was stunned but not daunted. She ran. There wasn't anything else she could do. She was too small and alone she knew she could not fight a full grown troll, or actually not even a baby one. She thought about it but good sense won through. Trolls are the biggest, nastiest and most evil creature she knew about.

That there was an unwelcome one in the secret garden that hadn't been repelled by the security spell was unthinkable. All she was thinking as she ran away with the troll in pursuit was that it shouldn't be there. But it was and although her magic was strong she couldn't use it on the troll. The magic protecting the garden was outrageously strong so the magic that had allowed such a creature past its defences must be equally strong.

The troll grunted and thought about chasing the small creature but he wasn't interested in Frixian meat. Frixian was too clothy and the spirit inside was incorporeal so of no use to a Troll. He also couldn't remember now what his instructions had been. He knew he had been given some but all he knew was that he could smell goat, he loved to eat goat and all else didn't matter.

His big feet stepped effortlessly across the stream and he stepped up the bank without breaking stride. His big feet sunk into the soft earth but he carried on quickly. Foot step after foot step he left a distinctive print with every step, a very deep print. He passed the dog kennels and ignored their barking. They were locked in their kennels and anyway he didn't like food that would bite him back. Bites can get infected so as he didn't need to eat them he didn't bother with them.

He was famished. Travelling by magic always made him hungry and the boss was always sending him somewhere with nothing to eat. This must have been a lot of magic as he was very hungry.

He passed the aviaries full of caged meat. He didn't want duck as it was too bony and would only be a crunchy snack. He'd leave them for now. Perhaps later. He wanted goat.

His feet squelched in the mud and he could smell the little Frixian who had hidden to let him pass and was now sneaking along behind him. He knew that she was there. He also knew that her magic wouldn't be able to get through the protection the Witch had put on him. The little one was brave to follow him. He wouldn't kill her yet, she was amusing. He'd play with her later.

He looked about the field and saw the big stone goat barn. He passed between the barn and the disused pig sty, ripped the door off and stuck his head through the now open doorway.

A creamy white goat looked up in surprise. Her long droopy ears hung down either side of an elegantly long nose with the recognisable Anglo Nubian curve. Her long sleek legs ended in neat hooves. She wasn't as fat as he would have liked but she would do. He wasn't choosy, he preferred to eat the first goat as they were usually the most trouble if left and then see what he fancied after that.

Beside her was a brown and black billy goat who also had long floppy ears. He ran away. A black and white goat with a crazy curved horn stub bleated in a stunned fashion before he too ran away to the back of the pen.

He looked at the three and decided he was right, as always, the first goat was best. He reached forwards and ripped the metal gate off of its hooks before throwing it out of the door. It bounced and rolled and narrowly missed the little Frixian who was sneaking up behind him.

The troll reached forward and grabbed at the creamy white goat but she was too fast, remarkably fast. She leapt to the back of her pen so his big fist closed on empty air.

In the next pen a black goat with snowy ears and white spots like stars on his coat bleated a very human "No".

The troll was stunned by this. The black goat then leapt easily out of his pen as if the gate wasn't there. It was only goodwill that kept him there anyway. He leapt to stand beside his mother the cream goat. The two of them faced the troll which bemused the troll as he would have expected them to have run away.

The troll then laughed. "So you both want to be eaten. Alright, I think I can manage that. You aren't too fat. Don't worry the rest of you. I'll have plenty of room for you. When I have ripped the flesh from the bones of these two."

He reached again for the white goat but as his huge fat hand with gnarly fingers closed around her elegant neck a bright light blasted him backwards.

He flew back out of the goat house. Widget dived aside as he nearly hit her on the way out. The troll landed on his big backside in the mud. He hit his head on the fence post and as he rubbed it a tall woman elegantly dressed in a cream dress drifted out of the goat house. She floated above the straw, her neat satin ballet shoes keeping clean. Her gossamer gown floated and glowed in the breeze. Her impossibly thin wings fluttering to keep her tiny feet away from the mud.

Her son was at her side. He was still a goat but now he had large black leathery wings which were neatly folded against his back. They twitched slightly as he strode out of the shed with her. He stood defiant, his horns held proud, his wings now flapping gently as he walked forward with his mother towards the troll.

Stormcrow, the spotted goat, leapt past the troll and landed next to Widget who climbed onto his back. Together they took to the air. Widget waved to the white lady. "Thank you Frixie Pfriend".

The woman bowed her elegant neck. Her golden blonde hair silkily soft.

Her eyes were gentle despite the situation. "Leave this place you foul beast. You have no place here. You do not belong here. You will eat no goats in this place."

The troll stood up as he rubbed his head. He sniffed the air and looked around. Then he laughed and leapt into the neighbours' field where two pygmy goats were quietly grazing. One had an old break in her leg that had not been bound so her leg was healed bent so as her friend ran away she had difficulty keeping up.

Widget grabbed hold of the ruff of her goat's neck as she knew what was coming next. "Stormcrow, we must protect our friends".

Stormcrow flapped his leathery wings and took to the air. He flapped and flapped his wings and built up speed just as the troll caught up with the little disabled pygmy goat. Widget was hanging on for grim death as Stormcrow put his head down and butted the troll on his backside. The troll howled, was off balance and so surprised that he tumbled and fell forwards onto the grass. Widget regained her balance as she had very nearly fallen off. She uttered a few words and concentrated as best she could as Stormcrow flew around the troll. As she spoke the words and the troll raised up into the air. She held him there, spinning like a top. "Ok Frixie Pfriend, what do I do now?"

Frixie looked at the spinning troll and laughed. The sound was like silvery bells ringing and her bleat could be heard across the valley.

Widget looked at her in desperation. "I mean it, my arm is aching. I can't hold the troll in the air forever."

The troll was getting closer and closer to the ground and the pygmy goat realised that the troll was far too close. She began to run as fast as her three legs could carry her.

The troll got closer and closer to the ground. As he almost touched down he grinned and slapped his fist into his other hand. "Now I will eat you all."

His feet nearly touched the ground as he heard a snort

from the door of the goat house. Brenin the Arapawa buck had jumped the gate of his pen and came thundering out of the shed. He leapt the stream and snorted at the fence, knowing he could not jump it.

Frixie Pfriend raised her hand and Brenin was lifted off his feet, carried across the fence and landed on the other side. He was not phased by this, he was too angry. He took off at a gallop.

His hooves thundered on the grass as he built up momentum. His huge handlebar horns were all that the troll could see approaching at quite a speed.

There was a snort and Orpheus the brown buck goat without horns leapt out of his pen, leapt the stream and Frixie Pfriend lifted him across the fence as well.

The troll looked for something to hold onto but there was nothing. He kicked his legs, they kicked in empty air. He reached for the ground, it was too far away. Widget was struggling but she managed to keep him just above the ground with the last of her strength.

Brenin hit him at full pelt with his head down and his determination steely. He gave the troll all he could and the troll soared into the air. As he did this Frixie Pfriend opened a portal in front of him and the troll flew helplessly through it. It closed in silence behind the troll and he was gone.

Brenin snorted and shook his coat, sorting out his fur. He stamped his foot on the ground and reeled around the bowed his noble head. He stood up on his back legs and bowed his head to Frixie Pfriend. His eyes were dark and excited for a moment. Then he trotted across the grass and waited at the fence to be lifted back.

Once he was back on the other side he trotted back to the pen where he was greeted by his Arapawa girlfriend and daughters.

Stormcrow flew back to the area outside the goat shed so that Widget could climb off. She threw her arms around him and he bowed his neck around her. "You are my goat, my special goat now."

Orpheus was also returned to his shed where he lived with Frixie Pfriend. The gate floated back into place and hay from the barn floated out and filled the hay rack attached to the gate as their hay had spilled into the mud. He walked calmly to the rack and began eating.

Frixie drifted over and stood beside Widget. Her voice was gentle. "The power of three billy goats is of course legendary when one is dealing with trolls."

Widget smiled. "Indeed it is. But Frixie, I didn't know you could do that. I thought you were a goat."

Frixie smiled. "There is a lot about me that you do not know and there is no need to know. You are quite correct, I am not a goat. I am an ancient fey of this realm but I took on the form of a goat a couple of years ago in order to live my life in the way I wanted to. You know my son, Stormcrow. He is half faerie, half goat. He is indeed Orpheus' son, before Orpheus gets worried and I am very proud of him."

Widget looked confused. "Are you all faeries or goats?"

Frixie smiled kindly. "They are goats. Wonderful, marvelous goats."

Widget signed. "Well a few more like you wouldn't go amiss. It looks like we are going to have more problems. Was that Goblian magic that let him in here?"

Frixie thought about it for a moment. "I don't think they have the power. That magic was ancient evil dark magic. It was Goblian as well. It feels like a massive amount of Goblians adding their power together. Mainly I felt the dark force though fuelled by anger, disappointment and loneliness. That sort of power comes from someone who is ancient and gets twisted by their past from what have been a good person to a bad one. They are the most dangerous as they are spiteful and harmful."

Widget looked worried. "We can't fight power like that. Not just us. I have never met anything like it."

Frixie looked sad. "I know, which is why you are going to have to open up that gateway in your secret garden for now. It isn't a full gateway, it is one that was created by a departing Frixian. One day you will find a real one or create a real one but for now that will have to do. That is what the Goblians were looking for I would hasten to guess. They could use it, not that they need it. It would stop the Frixians and multiply the number of their forces that they can bring into the world.

It is quite simple. Whoever can open the gateway would have a great advantage. It is a portal to your home world and it would mean that your people could come through quickly and in great numbers."

Widget looked thoughtful. "Does it open easily?"

Frixie shook her head. "It is stepped out of time. You need to link something now with something when it was locked and hopefully that will pull it into your time. I am only guessing. I could be very wrong but the Weaver sent me a dream and I have interpreted it that way. But, I am only a goat now." She laughed. "Whatever you see of the gateway is of this world, not yours. I can't hold this form in your realm much longer so I'm not going to be able to help you. We are glad the Weaver of Dreams is back. She will help you. Listen to your dreams and make sure that you make time to dream them. Instinct tells me that you are going to have to fix your TAVERN to get that portal open. Or if you can find some other way to travel around in time and space that might be quicker.

My power is fading. I am hungry and I want hay. So I will bid you farewell. My son and I must return to our shed and our eating." As she finished speaking she became the goat again and Stormcrow's wings faded into mist.

Widget tidied up the mess in the goat house and returned to the secret magical garden. She spent nearly an hour looking around, turning leaves, feeling for solid bits under the leaves. Finally she found what she could be looking for. It looked like a drain cover and she hoped that it wasn't. It was in the corner of the garden and it made no sense so that was her reasoning. Why put a cover where there wouldn't be a drain. It was out of place and she had a good feeling about that. She pulled and pulled despite being a little scared and finally she managed to lift it up and flip it over using a branch to lever it. But, there was nothing underneath, just earth. This made her more sure it was the gateway as it was pointless.

"Now what to do" She said to herself.

Siouxsie Sioux was walking past and her miaow sounded like. "Get yourself something and start digging."

Widget jumped. "Is anyone normal around here?"

Siouxsie purred. "Define normal." Before she strode off looking for mice.

Widget went to the metal feed shed and found herself a trowel. She went back to the disturbed earth and began to dig. She dug and dug and as the hole got bigger she began to wonder if she was doing the right thing. As the hole got bigger her enthusiasm got smaller. She dug a little more and was wondering if she should stop. Just then trowel struck something metal.

She then dug with more enthusiasm and found a small metal box. It was deeply embedded in the earth so she had to dig around it but finally she could pull it out.

The box lay on the grass in front of her covered in sticky earth and looking like a dirty box. She frowned and tried to open it. To her surprise it did open and inside there was a small piece of paper. There was writing on the paper so she read it.

"To whom it may concern,

If you are a Frixian then you can read this. Then you know this already as you are reading this. If you are a Goblian then you can't be reading this as you will already have been blown to oblivion and this paper would be back in the box. So that was a pointless statement.

At this point I should mention that any reasoning that this could be used to blow up Goblians is flawed as it only works in this area and is intended to keep them away from the gateway.

So, if you are reading this, Congratulations.

I left this message just in case we needed to open the gateways again. I closed this gateway on the 13th December 1972. Mankind was getting dangerously close to finding a gateway on the Moon and to avoid this we had to close all gateways. If they haven't been back to the moon and it was an over reaction then what the heck. They were showing far too much interest in the dark rock which had indicated an eruption in the past in their minds. We were worried that a further visit to the moon would take them closer to the volcanic site where they would find the gateway. I also lost the key. Sorry.

If it is essential for you to open the gateway then this can be done by taking a time travelling device back in time to that date. On that date you should bring some of that rock to earth. Don't let them see you.

It is easy enough, wait until they are gone. There is a metal in that rock which can be used to forge a key that will open the gateway. On the bottom of this note is a time and place to go and place the metal from the rock. That metal will then be used to make a key and that will be the key that you need. The key to justice is the key to the gateway as well."

Widget put the empty box back in the hole and covered the soil back in. She replaced the drain cover and walked back to the house full of thoughts and confusion. She went inside and sat down on her small Frixian size chair in the corner under the stairs that had been set up for her and thought and thought. She wished that Gadget was there but she could hear her moving around upstairs.

She sighed and climbed off of her chair again and went into the TAVERN where Elir, one of the Pixie Band, was working on some wiring. She looked up as Widget came in and smiled. "Hello there, you look worried. Sit down."

Elir went into her quarters and came back with a big pot of coffee and two mugs which she handed to Widget. "Sit down, tell me all about it and we'll see if we can come up with an answer."

Widget sat at a bench and lifted Elir up onto the table where she sat down and crossed her legs.

Widget took a deep breath, a mouth full of coffee and when she had swallowed it she thought a moment and then spoke. "We have found a gateway. If we can open the gateway then we can bring more Frixians to Earth.

To do that we have to go back in time and do something. We need to fix the TAVERN."

Elir shook her head. "The control box is gone, not just broken."

Widget looked confused. "What do you mean gone?"

Elir took a deep breath and sighed. "Kevin, who helped us to recreate the TAVERN took the box back to his home to do some work on it as he couldn't spend the time here. He lost his house and had to store things in a garage. The control box was kept there too as he didn't have room for it where he was. Things were stolen from the garage, they stole the control

box."

Widget looked horrified. "That is serious."

Elir nodded agreement. "Indeed it is."

Widget shook her head. "But to a human it would have looked like a plastic box with some old circuit boards and a few flashing lights. Without the Frixian magic and holographic element I cannot see what anyone would want with it. How are we going to communicate with the TAVERN now?"

Elir was looking at her hands. "We can fix it but it would take getting a lot of equipment together. If the Goblians influenced the thieves to take the box then so be it. We can't get it back. We can build another but not in the near future."

Widget thought for a moment. "Well if we can't use this device we will have to find another. I was watching the television the other day and there is another device, the Tardis."

Elir laughed. "That is a television show. It isn't real."

Widget looked serious. "What a great cover story and in any case in one dimension or the other that machine will exist as there are people out there who believe it does. That is enough. All I have to do is to get to it and normally I would say that is impossible as it is a television prop. But, I happen to know that there is a way that I can not only touch it I can walk around it. There is an incarnation of it in the Dr Who Exhibition in Cardiff. Even more coincidental I know that Angel, Niall and Sarah are going there for their birthdays and Christmas shopping. They are going to be walking around it and it won't take much to convince them to take me with them. Basically, I'll tell them the truth."

Elir shook her head. "You can wind me up sometimes but sometimes you come up with the right thing. If you can get an alternative machine then you might also be able to fix the TAVERN if you can pick up some equipment for me at the same time."

Widget laughed. "If I could go back and get the box I would but that would damage the time space continuum. I can however pick up the parts that will make another one. But I could do that in this world at this time so there would be very little point."

Elir thought about it. "We don't have Kevin this time but I am not sure that the human element is totally necessary. It was great to get it started but I think we can manage ourselves."

Widget thought for a moment. "Lots of thinking to do but there is one solution I can think of. I could borrow the Tardis to go home. When I get there I will be able to look for some of the Elahais Crystals. They would power the new control box. There are a couple from the old one but certainly not enough. The majority of them were in the box that Kevin took with him to Telford. I could hunt down the thieves and take it back but that could end up in a negative action."

Elir smiled. "You don't need to. That box needs to be discharged occasionally or power builds up in the crystals. I didn't need to tell Kevin that as he was working on it and I had it on a remote connection to here. When they took the box they disconnected that connection. The box will inevitably be charged beyond its capacity to contain the power and it will explode. We might know where it was but there won't be anything worth recovering so you might as well forget it and make a new one."

A few days later Widget was getting ready to go to Cardiff. The morning had been exciting. There was a lot of rushing around and last minute packing. Once it was all packed the bags were put in the car and Widget sat on the back seat of Niall's BMW, the seatbelt keeping her in place. Gadget had stayed behind to look after the house and the goats. Thomas, a local boy who helped out around the place, was coming to do the feeding and everyone was catered for.

It was a two hour journey via Swansea and past Neath but to Widget it seemed to last a lifetime. She was looking out of the window but other than a blur of green she wasn't really interested. All she could think about was her home world and going home and wondering what that would be like now.

She was lost in her own world of thought. There was

no way of knowing what would happen and of course there would be Goblians to contend with. She was leaving her home territory so there would be no home protection for her.

I am Widget, I'll cope, she thought to herself. I am glad that I told Angel what I am going to do. I also can't believe that she emailed the Exhibition, told them about my writing and my visit and basically asked them if it was alright to borrow the Tardis while asking for permission to take pictures and put them in a book. What a good idea as I can expect no questions and it is perfectly safe for her to bring me into the exhibition without me ending up in the cloakroom. They no doubt think she is a self published author and that the book won't go anywhere so isn't worth worrying about.

That will be useful as I can't walk around in the Exhibition in the puppet or I would be seen. So I'll have to rely on being carried around. Frixian magic should hopefully let me use the Tadis and if it is a time traveling device then it will be slightly out of phase so I can move around and touch it as a Frixian.

The sun beat down on the silver car as it streaked towards Cardiff. The green grass flew past the window as Cardiff got closer. Cardiff, a city in the throws of its Christmas season with all the bright lights and shop keepers hopeful of earning their keep.

Children full of wonder as they see the white and sparkling world of imagery that will take them from their normal mundane lives. All oblivious to the threat that hung in the shadows on the periphery of every sparkly exhibition. The Goblians will be there, waiting for the child who is spoilt or angry. That is the child that will give them the strength to hurt others. The others that are hurt then become angry and vicious and the Goblians get stronger. In the consumer hell that is Christmas the Goblians have plenty of sustenance. The spoilt child that already has too much and who wants more and the child whose family are doing the best for them and who will be nevertheless disappointed because of expectations created by advertising. A beautiful old pagan time of simplistic ceremony has been hijacked by the modern world. Where in the rush to buy the perfect present is the baby Jesus?

Happy faces of the children on Christmas morning leads to the worried faces of the adults when the credit card bill comes in once the tinsel and pine needles have gone away. Where is Santa in that? That aged old elf who worked so closely with The Toymaker in the past now a commercial icon and decoration. Not that he looks like the fat old man in a red coat of course and the elves, well the magic of them is that the can appear as they want to appear.

Then again Christmas Day in many places is one day

when the world is in union. One day where very few people work and many spend time with family they don't see all year. A beautiful time of love and peace all tied up in a big red tinsel bow.

The car drew into Cardiff and they relied on the satellite navigation system which got them completely lost.

They passed the tall silver tower which had Torchwood underneath it. Widget couldn't help wondering and expected to see Captain Jack Harkness wandering down the road as they passed it by and went on down the road to their hotel which was outside the Bay itself.

Near it was the Millennium Centre in all its elegant practicality and after a drive up and down the road and a few wrong turns they were at the hotel. It wasn't quite where they had expected it to be and certainly further from the Bay than was useful. It was not quite what they were expecting either. They had seen the picture in the advertisement for the hotel but that photograph had obviously been taken from the other side and looked as though it was on the Bay, it wasn't. It was on a river and as they approached from the car park it looked like a care home. The Holiday Inn, Cardiff Bay was a bit misleading as it certainly wasn't on the Bay. Well it was nearly on the Bay but quite a walk and that wasn't what they had wanted. They had all hoped it would at least have a view of the Bay. For Widget in particular her hopes of sitting in the window and watching people enjoying themselves on the Bay were dashed.

The big glass doors were functional and clean, not really welcoming. The hotel inside was again plain and practical. Impersonal and very office like.

The staff however were friendly enough but it did lack any finesse.

There was no restaurant that they could see. Part of the bar had seating with practical school like tables which looked like it could be used as a restaurant. Not somewhere to actually enjoy, more a practical place to eat. Plain and functional, that was the bedroom as well, small and with a shower.

There were no mini soaps and that sort of thing but there was tea and coffee. It was only a base and somewhere to put things and as Widget thought about it as they carried her into the room, that was probably what it was for. It would be ideal for the businessman on a basic trip who had to stay over but she didn't want to spend a holiday there.

They were short on time as they had decided not to arrive the night before. With only one day to do everything it was therefore a bit of a rush. One day only for the Goblians to attack them though, that had to be a bonus. Being on Facebook and people knowing we were going meant that at the last minute they had decided not to go for both nights. That way if anyone was planning anything then they would be disappointed.

Widget sat on a chair for a while as Niall, Angel and Sarah met up down in the reception area. She looked around as carefully as she could. It was a strange place to her and felt a bit like a railway station. It had an odd atmosphere which was probably to do with people coming and going. It also smelt odd, dusty and smelt of Goblian.

Then there was a flurry and no time to be lost. Bags were left unopened, mobile phone calls were made and after a couple of drinks at the bar to relax Niall after the drive the taxi was ordered to take them all to the Dr Who Exhibition.

Now Widget was beginning to feel nervous. It was the moment of truth.

They were so close now.

Originally they had hoped that they could walk to the Exhibition and the Bay. The truth was that they needed a taxi to get to both.

The taxi drew up and they climbed inside. Widget was in her basket as that was the easiest way to carry her and she flopped down and looked just like a rag doll puppet. She didn't see the houses and shops passing by the car but she could listen and all she was concentrating on was listening out for the distinctive sound of Goblians.

The taxi drove through the wasteland around the Exhibition that looked like it was waiting for more things to be built. As it was winter it was a bit desolate but as Widget sneaked a peek she was reassured to see a model of a crashed Tardis outside the exhibition and she couldn't help but wonder. As she was going to borrow a vehicle she didn't know how to drive and as she was going to time and space travel was she going to crash it in the past and was that the result of her trip? Time travel can be a tricky thing.

She took a deep breath as Angel got out of the car and picked her up in the basket. All she could think about was that she wasn't fun Widget today, she was serious. This was going to be serious and very dangerous.

The glass doors along the outside of the Exhibition were fascinating as behind them they could see the costumes that had been used in various of the episodes. They were very welcoming and the place wasn't busy so that was reassuring as well. If anything went wrong then there weren't too many people to get hurt. They stepped inside and it felt like leaving the mundane world behind.

Still wondering about the crashed Tardis Widget was glad to be distracted by the costume exhibition in the foyer.

Inside was very like a cinema foyer. There was a pleasantly laid out café and the models around it did give it a very amusing décor. It was a lovely place to sit with friends and chat before it was time to go into the Exhibition. To Widget they were dangerous, she could feel a threat, as they could harbour Goblians hiding inside just waiting to attack. Goblian magic could also inhabit them and make them move, that was also dangerous. She couldn't help thinking that nothing was safe anymore. Goblian magic was in the air.

Knowing that the few who were coming along were roleplayers was also reassuring as they would be able to cope. They also knew what Widget was up to, even if it was only that she was visiting the Exhibition to make what was going to be written about in a book more real, made everything easier. She knew that they had the gift of imagination and could see beyond the mundane. They understood Science Fiction and loved it. That would hopefully help if anything went wrong.

Widget was trying to think it through. She could

understand that she was a magical creature and anything in the Tardis would have an element that was magical because of the particles picked up when travelling. Magic being logical, chemical and physical and mathematics based. People who have a creative mind have the ability to understand and use this. She realised as she waited that she could probably get any of them to help her. That was something to keep in mind. When it came to it she didn't know how things were going to go.

She looked around the group who were happily chatting. Somehow she didn't believe that they believed that she was an alien in a puppet. She did believe that it was a roleplaying situation and that it was a pretend that she was an alien in a puppet so they were reacting to the puppet. For her part it didn't matter as long as the result was the same.

The exhibits glared at them and it was easy to imagine them moving.

Perhaps that was why they were there, to add to the excitement. The time ticked by like an impossibly slow beast and that meant that Widget had to keep watch until she was almost exhausted. Every small movement made her concentrate.

Finally it was time to go into the Exhibition. Tick, tock the clock had ticked and now they were going. Widget was still in the basket, trapped as she couldn't be seen to move. Angel picked it up and they all went to the cloak room where they could leave their coats. She put the basket down and for one nasty moment Widget thought that she was going to be left behind.

Not that it mattered too much as she knew that she would have to do the journey without the puppet body. When she got into the Tardis she would have to be Frixian, the cloth body would be set aside but she really didn't want to lose it. Having the control box stolen had upset her, losing her body would be much more upsetting.

She had planned and planned it in her mind but as they got nearer to the entrance she began to panic. She didn't know how this would go but she knew whatever happened she had to get it right. Before the people got into the Exhibition she would have to borrow the Tardis, use it and return it. She didn't know exactly how it as going to happen but as they neared the door she realised that she could feel the magic on the door. If the door was open she could get through and that was her opportunity.

As she stepped out of her body she really wished that The Doctor was actually there to help her. His help would have been so useful but for now he would have to just loan his Tardis, whether he realised it or not. Whether he existed or not in this dimension was irrelevant as he did exist in another. As dimensions can cross then his existence in any dimension merely depends on where he is at the time. Though most things don't cross over, just images of them or on the rare occasion the whole entity.

She had to be quick as the whole plan relied on getting into the room before anyone else to give herself the maximum amount of time to look around and get her bearings and actually find the Tardis.

Step, step, timing, words from all around her she couldn't hear because she was concentrating so hard and the door opened to the Exhibition. That was her time to go. The Tardis' defences were down so that the public could get in. That was her opportunity as normally the Tardis would have bounced her right out of the door.

She took a deep breath and the Frixian Spirit reached out of the puppet, her legs stretching to the ground, her body growing from the three foot of the puppet to the six foot tall shape that is a Frixian.

She was then between the two dimensions and she then saw the Goblians up against the glass outside the front window of the Exhibition. There were hundreds of them.

She began to run. The door was solid so she had to get through while the employee held it open, before the outer defences closed and she had to hope that the

Tardis didn't pick her up on its sensors. She pushed past people who didn't notice as everyone was pressed together anyway and she avoided contact as much as she could before stepping through the door.

There is was, the Tardis in all its glory. Lights flashing, colours dark and blue and alien. It was powered up for the forthcoming show, it was powered up for Widget.

She leapt to the controls and pushed the levers that she needed to push. Hours of watching the DVDs paid off as she knew what to do.

She was still hoping that The Doctor would turn up. The pre recorded show for the visitors started when Widget activated the controls and there was his face but it shut down again as soon as she put the Tardis into non display action.

There was the familiar whiz, whiz, scrapey, scrapey sound. The Tardis shifted in time and space and then there was nothing, silence. It was a serene moment of knowing that the Tardis had moved before having to do anything about it. It was then that she noticed a pair of gloves hanging over a chair. With a grin she grabbed them and put them on.

Widget opened the door. Outside the moon was cold, the chill blew into the Tardis as soon as the door opened. Widget stepped outside, shut the door and looked around.

In the distance she saw a moon vehicle heading back to Earth. It had blasted off and was on its way. Widget sighed with relief that she had got the timing right. All she could hope for was that it was the right day but everything seemed to be right.

Being ethereal the non gravity wasn't anything to worry about. She was able to walk without being launched out into space. Being ethereal she also didn't need to breathe and she was easily strong enough to counteract the pull on the gloves.

She walked carefully to the area of dark rock she had been expecting to see and as she was wearing the gloves she could pick up some pieces. She piled them up and then grabbed them in a pile in the cup of her hands and walked back to the Tardis.

Once back in the Tardis she altered the controls and set the dials. She activated the Tardis and it leapt into life. The noise sounded and then silence, she was at her destination.

Widget sighed, took a deep breath to keep calm and walked to the door. She put her hand on the door and opened it.

The doors flew open and the purple light of her home filled the Tardis. The smell of flowers was intense.

Heady waves of it wafted into the interior and mixed with the metallic aroma of the Tardis.

The mountains and hills that surrounded the valley where the Tardis had landed soared to impossible heights. The Tardis nestled neatly between two hillocks, perfectly landed, right where it was sheltered. But, there was no time for Widget to congratulate herself. This was the most dangerous part of her mission as she had to get the crystals that she needed. She was physical so picking them up wouldn't be a problem, she was physical so that could be a problem as anything could harm her.

How she longed to take some time and to go and see people she hadn't seen for so long. She really wanted to but she knew she couldn't. This was too important.

The soft springy grass of home was just as she remembered it. Stifling a tear she walked out into the open. The scent and feeling brought a warmth to her. She was so glad to be home. So pleased she didn't realise until too late that she had walked out of the hillock into a herd of lilac unicorns. They were as surprised as she was and galloped towards the mountain. That in turn spooked a baby dragon who was asleep under a tree. He took flight and soared into the sky which brought a stunned silence to the birds who had been singing.

The silence of the valley was destroyed in a moment. In the distance the sound of explosions and gunfire ringing out and echoing around the valley causing all the creatures to run for cover. The little dragon's scales reflected the lilac light as he soared into the heavens.

In the distance the distinctive sound of battle rang out. Explosions were almost regular but in the next valley, not the valley that Widget was in. Out there the war was raging but it had for years, not this close though. The valley was under threat, this was far too close for comfort. She realised as she thought about it that the valley was probably the last bastion of fantasy and hope. If the people of Earth still believed in magic then the protection could hold and the valley might survive.

What happens on Earth always has had an effect on what happens in the other realms as they technically share the same space and time. Like echoes in the Universe the dimensions all exist together at the same time. It brought it home. Protecting Earth was protecting her home planet. If the Goblians won on Earth they would win here.

The Frixians needed the crystals as much as The Doctor did for his Tardis. Both need crystals from the planet that Widget called home. They were grown there and nowhere else so she decided to bring an extra crystal back for The Doctor and perhaps then he may forgive her for borrowing the Tardis.

She whispered. "Words are spoken, out of sight. Whispered, broken, to find what is right. The words I whisper they seem to boom out. Although they are quiet, gently that's right. That is magic, it has no concept of volume." She spoke to nobody in particular, so conscious that she was on her own.

There was only a moment to wait and then the ground began to glow in places. The crystals glowing as they heard her voice.

It took nearly an hour and she dug and dug. It took longer as she needed to keep a very careful eye on what was going on around her. One by one she dug up the crystals and put them into a little bag.

Then she smelt it, Goblian magic. It was strong and stinky. A dark smell cloud in the eternity of beautiful scents from the plants and flowers. Goblians were close. The war was spilling into the valley and in Widget's mind that couldn't happen. This was far too soon, she needed more time. She wasn't ready and the whole awfulness of the situation bore down on her.

A fireball crackled through the air, heading towards the Frixian. Huge, black, glowing red and burning. She didn't panic. She held her hand up and the magic flowed. She tried to hold it in mid air but the power that had sent it was too strong. She could only slow it so that it fell short of her. It missed her and the Tardis but the once beautiful foliage and animals it landed on as it bounced disappeared in a flower of fire.

A black creature rose up from behind the mountain where the battle was raging and swooped down. It was a bird but very lizard like. Not a dragon but similar. It had huge leathery wings which flapped regularly, holding it in the air. Its talons were sharp and poised ready to grab. There were no points for what its razor sharp beak was intent on doing, it was ready to bite. On its back it carried a Goblian. He was dressed head to foot in black spiked armour as one hand grasped the rope which guided the creature, the other holding a poised barbed trident.

Widget thought to herself that she would have to have enough crystals. She grabbed the last of them that she could reach and stuffed them into the bag and her pocket as the bag was full.

As the beast bore down on her she could only run. She didn't hesitate, she ran as fast as she could. She didn't look back, she just ran fast, leapt through the Tardis' open door which slammed shut behind her.

She was glad to be safe from the creature but she was equally glad to shut out the sound of the animals and plants screaming in pain.

Widget was out of breath. "Now that was close. They can't be there, they just can't be. This was the last secure place, this is my home. Those poor animals. What about my family and other people. What can I do?"

There was no answering voice. At that moment she really wanted The Doctor to appear from a corridor but there was nobody. She was alone in the Tardis.

"Oh well, I'll talk to you Tardis and pretend that you can hear me.

I have a problem, the planet has a problem. The darkness in mankind's hearts and minds is reflected here, destroying the beauty and the peace. War for mankind means power for the Goblians and they must have a lot of power now. I have been sitting on my mountain believing that all we had to do was provide a sanctuary. Sanctuaries aren't immune to the sort of damage that men can do. It has all been quiet for too long. There is a world of pain out there and mankind has forgotten what living without it is all about. Simple kindness to others. If that was what everyone was like there would be no pain and sorrow.

As I have the Tardis I think I had better use you to get to the time and place on Earth where I can speak to the Weaver of Dreams. She will know what to do. I think I may have to borrow you a little bit longer. I am sure nobody will mind as although they have no choice I should have you back before they know you are gone. Unless I get killed but then I won't have to answer for borrowing you.

Ok Tardis, take me to the Weaver. Ok, now I have to remember which levers to pull." She thought about it and pulled four levers and set them in a position she hoped was right.

"So now I have to find some clothes as the proximity to the Weaver of Dreams will give this body a physical form on Earth and I wouldn't want to be naked. I hope you don't mind if I borrow some. I will return them. I know that you have a great wardrobe and I should be able to find something that I like."

The Tardis ground into action and phased out of time and space. It spiralled through the eons and dimensions and returned to Earth.

The Tardis came to rest on a windswept hillside beside a pile of rocks in a place known as Dynas Emrys in North Wales. The door opened and a tall woman with curly black hair and alabaster skin stepped out from inside. Her hair blew in the wind, her black tail coat flapping slightly and her frilly white pirate shirt was ruffled by the breeze too.

Obviously she wore a bowtie as bowties are cool but not as a tie, around her neck as a necklace. Harlequin patterned multi coloured leggings were a stark contrast to the sombre black jacket and white shirt but while choosing something practical yet outlandish she could not resist them. A pocket watch that she had also found there went well with the ensemble she thought. She had thought about a walking cane, it would have set off the outfit, but discarded the idea. She couldn't however resist the silken top hat although she had adorned it with a piece of wide black lace and added a few brooches to make it more feminine. As magic was no object she had also attached some watch cogs and other bits and pieces to the jacket, just so that it looked a bit more special.

She smiled as that was the wonder of time travel. She had been able to take as much time as she liked getting there and arrived a split second after she set off. She had taken a swim in the swimming pool, had dinner, wandered about, made an outfit and generally enjoyed stretching her limbs in a physical way after being ethereal and trapped in a puppet for so long.

It had been a lovely break but now it was time to face reality again and get on with the mission.

As her laced up Victorian boots stepped out onto the

soft grass she wondered if something more robust would have been more appropriate. It was not time for a wardrobe malfunction. Also, as she stepped out into the chilled wind she really wished she had selected a warm coat to go with the outfit as there were plenty there.

She sighed, thinking better to get on with it now and turned, shut the door and took the key out of the lock and put it in her pocket. She patted the pocket as if to feel it there and to reassure herself that it was safe. She then had second thoughts, took it out of her pocket and attached it to the clasp on her watch chain.

She had had hours to get used to being physical again but as she felt the wind on her skin she really felt alive. All her senses were taking in the smells, feelings and atmosphere of the wild Welsh weather.

The landscape was still green but clearly in the throws of winter. The grass had less lustre and the trees had discarded their autumn colours. The wind had a chilled smell to it and the whole aspect of the place was grey.

With the Tardis behind her but within running distance she approached a tall stone. It wasn't large enough to count as a standing stone in the true sense. Then there was a dilemma, what to do? She thought about it and called "Weaver of Dreams". Nothing happened. She thought about it again, put her hand on the rock and called again. This time not in words, she projected the words as she did when she communicated with Angel.

A crack appeared in the stone, silently it spread and widened until it was large enough for her to walk through. The stone itself had grown to towering proportions. She didn't hesitate for to do so would be rude. She took a deep breath and stepped through the crack which immediately closed with a gentle stone on stone tap behind her. It was pitch black for a moment and she reached for her torch which she had thought to put in her pocket but she didn't need it. As her eyes became used to the light she realised that the area was lit with an ambient light which was enough to look around and to walk by.

She was in a small carved stone cave. It was unadorned and unremarkable other than being there at all. It was no more than ten feet in diameter. A spiral staircase opened up at its center point and there was no doubt which way she had to go.

Down she went, step by step, deep into the earth. Her boots made a distinctive click, click with every step which sounded tumultuous in the silence. The further down she went the more the white ambient light was replaced by a green glow from some sort of green moss which emanated it from stalks which grew up out of the velvety carpet of tiny fronds. The air was musty and damp the further down she went. Just how she had imagined ancient caverns to smell in the storybooks she loved so much.

Soon enough she reached the bottom of the stairs. The spiral opening up into another cave although this one was much larger and clearly natural. It was a good fifty feet long by about twenty five feet wide. She could never cope with working things out in the metric equivalent. A stream ran through it, cutting it into two distinct halves. Stalactites hung down, stalagmites reached up towards them. The droplets of water that had created them and which was still creating them making them glisten in the light from torches which were evenly spaced around the cave. At the back of the cave there were pillars created where these creations of nature had come together years ago.

The cavern smelt of incense and she could see cones and sticks burning on a small stone table. It was also warmer than she would have expected. Being better lit than the stairway she was able to look around and see everything. The number of torches made sure of that and it was likely that the heat was coming from them and the huge fireplace against the side wall. A roaring fire burnt in the grate, warming an area around it where sofas and a rug created a comfortable living area.

On the other side of the stream the cavern was bare of furniture. The only feature that stood out was an alcove. It was about five feet up the wall so easy to reach and it seemed to glow and call to her.

As she stepped forwards and off of the stairs she felt a chill as when she looked back the stairs were gone as were the fire and sofas.

She was not surprised somehow. She knew that this place was created by old magic, Dragon Magic, the Magic of the Dragon Kings. The last hall where they had once met.

Her feet were now bare, her boots were gone as she stepped forwards, her clothes had become her diaphanous gown again, her borrowed clothes lay on the floor where they had fallen from her.

She hesitated slightly but walked forward and stepped into the stream. It was all she could think of doing and as she wanted to talk to the Weaver so if that was what was required, that was what she was going to do.

As her feet touched the water her toes became claws. It was deeper than it looked and as she crossed she had to swim as it got too deep to walk. The stream also got wider, it had at least doubled. She hadn't noticed but as she swam her body had changed. She too was now a dragon. This seemed so comfortable to her that she hadn't noticed. Somehow she had an ancient memory that she was a dragon and she had been like this before.

The water had become impossibly deep and the stream had become impossibly wide. She kept swimming, determined to get to the other side. It was hard to swim so she let her scaly tail propel her through the water.

The water got shallower and she walked out of the water again and stood on the other side. She looked down, she was still wearing the tail coat and she was completely dry. The stream was gone and she was standing in an empty cave.

A golden light surrounded her and a peace she had never felt. She now had a dilemma. She was fascinated by the goblet but that wasn't what she as here for. As it was the only thing in the cave she decided that it would be a good idea to see what it was. It was a simple wooden goblet bound with metal bands around its rim, the stem and metal strips joined these bands, following the curve of the goblet. A golden glow surrounded it.

Her fingers touched the cup. It felt like a wooden cup. It was very, very old.

She picked it up and as she did so she heard a voice in her head. "A promise." A gold light shone like a torch from the top of it and reached to the ceiling and the world seemed to spin around her.

A huge gold dragon appeared in the cave. She hadn't noticed it before as her back was to the cave as she stood looking at the goblet in her hand.

The dragon watched Widget. Her eyes were gentle, the pupil a bar, like a goat's eyes. Her noble scaled head was lowered as she had a look at Widget.

Widget then realised something was behind her and turned around slowly. She felt like a kid caught with her hand in the parents' sweet jar and for a moment she was convinced that the dragon was going to eat her.

The dragon laughed. "Fear not, for today you have seen a great light and the people in darkness will see it again too if they would just look. The power of dreams, belief and hope is stronger than the darkness we are faced with now.

You are looking for a weapon when what you need is a dream and a belief. That is all you need. When people can set aside anger, selfishness and pride they will look for similarities rather than the need to fight each other. Then the Goblians will have no power."

Widget felt so very small. "How can that happen?"

The dragon laughed. "It will happen if they could

realise but also when they have a greater enemy that brings their petty day to day vanities into context."

Widget frowned. "I don't think I like the sound of that."

The dragon stood in silence, thinking. Then she spoke. "There was a time when a story made them be all that they could be. The stories seem unimportant now and many have been forgotten in the rush of the mundane and bright lights of technology and the need to see everything as it is and to have everything explained and documented. The need for analysis and naming, to understand and to dissect everything into its component parts to further understand it has set aside the power of belief. The simplicity of meaning is now lost on the children of today when in the past they had great power to teach. While they want more there will be greed, necessity is one thing, want is another. When a child was happy with one thing that they loved that one thing had power. The throw away society leaves many of your kind in Charity Shops and dare I say it where there are no tags which prove them fire resistant they are thrown away or given to dogs."

Widget shuddered.

A single tear ran down the dragon's face and fell to the ground where it exploded in a myriad of sparking lights.

Widget shook her head. "What can be done?"

The dragon smiled. "I am the Weaver of Dreams and dreams must return. When mankind dreams they are the strongest and best of all creatures. Dreams are aspirations without greed and gluttony."

Widget looked serene. "Can you do that?"

The dragon looked down and sighed. "For those with the imagination to visualize and the intelligence to understand then yes I can. For those with closed minds there is little hope. They are trapped. They have an anger because they are empty. Their only happiness is in the neat and tidy physical things around them which are heartless and pointless. That may sound odd to you. There is a big difference between keeping items which have been gifts and have happy memories and expensive things accumulated so that they are status symbols. They have no inner confidence so they have to compensate with a false pride and a deluded belief that they are only worth what other people see that they have. I don't know if I can combat that.

For now those who look will find the magic of the glade, the infinite majesty of the stars and the joy of the golden sun.

We must speak of Goblians. There is no quick fix there, no answer, no secret weapon other than by removing their food and empowering children so that they can be happy. I will not and cannot wipe them out as that would be an evil act in itself. That act would bring such desolation that you could not imagine. You see them as evil, they are just hungry. They were created because of that same ill will and use that energy so that it does not build up to devastating proportions. They are not a natural creation, they were created to use that excess energy. Before you ask, I don't know who or what created them, that is a big secret which may be one to discover one day as it may lead to the answer as to how to get rid of them. Then again, remove the energy and they will fade away.

Every time someone does a pointless angry act another Goblian is born. Every time someone is selfish or belittles another to add to their own personal power another Goblian is born, fully grown and hungry.

With the power of dreams back in the world and if you can get the gateway open then every genuine good word, every genuine and selfless good act and every kind thought will create an energy which a Frixian can use to come through the gateway.

I don't need to tell you but I will speak it as it needs to have power and there is power in all words. Unlike Goblians your kind, Frixians, cannot be born here or spring forth fully grown in a body that can effect this realm. You can travel here and as you know you arrive as a spirit. So my new friend there is very little we can do other than give people good dreams and ignore and set aside the selfish words of the Goblianites."

Widget looked confused. "I know most of what you say but what is a Goblianite."

The Weaver smiled. The room changed and the fire and sofas reappeared. She indicated a seat and she and Widget sat down. "Goblianites are humans who perpetually create Goblians by their selfish attitude. Of course they don't know that they are doing it. They are just going about their lives feeling proud that they have won verbal battles that didn't need to be won, uttered profanities that were intended to hurt others and generally done any acts that cause negativity. They are marked forever as a little bit of their soul is also taken to create the creature. That is the bit that wasn't known until recently.

Of course we can't stop bad things happening to people. We can give them hope and a way of dealing with it all. Out of every bad thing something good will come. Even if it is just support for each other and simple, selfless acts of kindness for a stranger."

Widget thought about it. "The world has become selfish. Good people have become insular when they could reach out and be happy with others. They have a choice and you have to show them that choice. They can be victims, they can victimize others as they have been victims or they can grow strong from using that experience to make them better people despite what others have done to them."

The Weaver nodded in agreement. "You have the crystals and you can power the TAVERN again. I foresee a move though. You will all have to leave your hillside as older powers are calling you. There is an ancient place you need to go to, possibly just for a short time. Don't worry, when you look it will find you.

Go and have adventures and bring back such stories that will give people a world beyond the mundane. Bring back stories and build a place of happiness wherever that may be. You will meet opposition as people won't understand you or what you are doing. You will be challenging their comfort zone as they have been creating Goblians for far too long.

You need to give people a belief in something beyond the mundane. A place where they can be themselves, love themselves and be.

However dark this world gets I hope that there will be writers who bring light to the world. I hope that they will keep on writing stories that show that people can be strong and support each other. A man alone is just a man. A man with friends stands like iron and can never be truly defeated if he is loved. A man with people around him who believe in him has an army. If he falls others will take up his flag and carry him until he is strong again.

Go and open that portal. Don't be afraid, the Frixians are waiting. Bring the Frixians to your world and bring the light back to the darkness. You will need to get the key and open the lock."

Widget was looking much more confident. "Where is the key?"

The Weaver smiled. "The key is the love of a mother who stood by her daughter through anything and everything. She is gone from this world but her love lives on. She believed in magic and fantasy and most of all she believed in her the daughter she was told she could never have. Her faith was rewarded by a daughter but it was her love and steadfastness after that which has given her the power even now. She has touched the key and that has given it power.

Her daughter's hand on that key as well gives it the magic so that it will open the gateway. A metal key is a metal key. It is as simple and as complicated as that. Angel can't put flowers on her mother's grave as it is too far away and her father's ashes were cast at sea so there is no grave there. Her father and her mother have touched that key, so has she. The key is in the TAVERN but unless you do what you need to do then it will just be a key. If that makes any sense. It is a time loop which is hard to understand I know. It is because you will do something, you will do something to make it more than what it already is. That will complete the magic and open the portal. Once done the time circle is complete.

It is all a circle. It is also Christmas in your world, the time of goodwill to all men. At this time you are at your strongest so this is the time to open the portal as very soon there will be gift bears in this world and they should have Frixians in them again. But, without the Toymaker you won't be able to bind the two. You may need the key but I will have to find a Toymaker for you.

It is all prepared for you to open the portal but it is only a temporary one.

It will have to move to an ancient place to have permanent power. It can open now because the Healing Circle is there. All that goodwill and energy sent by healers from all around the world is still there in those crystals, stored. It can all be used for the portal but it will run out in time.

Now is time for you to go. Your time here is done."

Widget breathed in and when she breathed out again she was back in the Tardis which was grinding its start up and moved.

Widget opened the door and knew immediately what she had to do. She was in a workshop which was obviously a forge. The Furness was glowing coals and the Blacksmith was sitting at a table where he had been eating is bread and cheese and enjoying a mug of tea. He had already looked up, stunned when the big blue box had arrived. Now he was equally stunned when a tall transparent woman in a floating dress wearing a pair of gardening gloves stepped out of it. His mouth was opening and closing and he was frozen to the spot.

Widget smiled. "Don't worry, I am not going to hurt you. You are about to make a key for Leyton Police Station. I want you to use this metal. It will need the furness a little hotter but it will pour like any other metal." The Blacksmith couldn't find the words.

Widget tried another kind smile. "Don't worry. You are dreaming this.

Where do you keep the metal that you are going to use to make the key?"

The Blacksmith's mouth slammed shut and he pointed to the bench where there was a chunk of metal waiting to make the key. Widget walked to the table and swapped the metals over. She smiled. "You didn't see this and they would think you mad if you told anyone."

She walked back to the Tardis, stepped inside, shut the door and the Tardis left.

The Blacksmith shook his head and decided that he was going to forget the whole incident. He forged the key, cooled it, wrapped it and sent it with his boy to deliver it.

Widget smiled, her back against the door. "Here's hoping that he just makes it.

Time to go back I think but not before I borrow a few things. I hope you don't mind but I need to take some things from your scrap store room.

It took her several months but time was irrelevant and by the time she had finished she had what was a control box made from scraps from the Tardis' store room.

When it was done she set the controls for the TAVERN, moved the Tardis and left the control box on the table for Elir to find. Widget got back into her cloth body just as Angel carried her into the Exhibition. Angel felt her arrive back. In her head she heard. "I'm back." She thought out the conversation. "How did it go?"

Widget smiled. "Very well thank you. I'm going to enjoy the Exhibition now but I'm not going to write about it, not while the Exhibition is current. It wouldn't be fair to spoil the surprise for the children who are going to visit.

It would spoil the magic."

They walked the Exhibition and enjoyed the whole trip of being invited to fly the Tardis. The atmosphere was wonderful and as they played through the scene everyone felt that they were truly flying the ship.

The Exhibition had been set out so that visitors could see the costumes set out as they walked down tunnels until they stepped out into a big room. Costumes were set out in groups to be looked at and props were able to be seen close up. It was cold though and that made it a little unpleasant.

Angel smiled and thought to Widget. "It has changed a bit, there is less here now. I read something that they have had to take some things from the Exhibition for filming. It is a shame but it is still good. The walk through bit seems a bit shorter as well. I came before when it was the Fiftieth Anniversary so perhaps it was more comprehensive then. Of course they have brought in Mr Capaldi's Doctor series props and costumes but I wish that there was a waxwork of him too. There are the other doctors but perhaps he will join them soon. I like it in general. They have taken from the Exhibition for their new music project as well. The music from the episodes is being put together with a live orchestra for an evening out. I looked it up on the internet. It is interesting, obviously a bit expensive and we have had our time away so it is unlikely that we can go.

A young man and woman who had been guiding people around and explaining things about the Exhibition came over to take a look at Widget. They were amused when it was explained that they were there to borrow the Tardis. It was irrelevant as they wouldn't see anything different and everything was the same, other than the crystal left for The Doctor. Of course if they did any checks they will see that it has a few more time miles on the clock.

Widget was greatly honoured when the lovely lady had her photo taken with her. It was a special moment for her and she really liked it. To be close to someone with so much enthusiasm for their job and the happiness that emanated was encouraging at a time when Widget needed it most.

She showed Widget her sonic screwdriver and this fascinated her. It was very special. She remembered that she had a little one which was a torch.

The Exhibition had the old Tardis incarnations, captured from time and space and held in a moment before they changed. The same of course was true of the current Tardis. It was taken out of time. The timeline had continued and it was also travelling with The Doctor.

Widget was lost in thought as they walked around the rest of the Exhibition. Sarah took some photographs but Widget hardly noticed. She was too busy wondering what would happen next and remembering the Goblians who were outside the main door.

Time passed and it was time to leave. They left the Exhibition and went back to the cloakroom and put their coats on. The Goblians were gone, they had not managed to get enough energy from the Exhibition as people were too happy so they had gone away.

It was time to go and everyone went back to their hotel rooms to get ready for the evening.

The night was dark and the lights were sparkling on the river. On any other night it would have been beautiful, even mystical. That night Widget was too afraid and that didn't make anything feel either beautiful or mystical. She had seen the television report that the police were on high alert in case of some terrorist action and you could feel the atmosphere that had caused.

Widget knew she was going to be left in the hotel room. She didn't like the idea but Niall and Angel rarely got time to themselves away from the animals so she understood. She wanted to be out in Cardiff looking around and having fun. But, Frixians are magical and she knew that she wouldn't be welcome as her presence could attract Goblians. It wouldn't be much fun for her either as whenever a human is around who can't believe then she would just be a cloth puppet and the thought of possibly sitting on dirty pub seats or getting something spilled on her was enough to make her want to stay in the hotel room anyway.

There had already been one accident, her wig was pulled off on one side where it had caught on Niall's jacket but that would easily be repaired when they got home. No, she would quietly sit, look out of the window and have some time to herself.

Widget was bored a quarter of an hour later. All her high ideals melted when there wasn't much on the television and there was nobody to talk to. It was also dark outside and she couldn't see anything interesting out there either.

She thought about leaving the room but if someone saw her then she would be stuck as a limp puppet and could be stolen or end up in the "Lost Property" and there would be some explaining to do.

She had to sit still and meditate and she thought about leaving the puppet and wandering around without it.

Her attention was dragged back into the room with a bump when she smelt Goblian. They were in the hotel and she knew that they were very close.

She went to the door, put her foot behind it and carefully opened it to take a look outside into the corridor. She braced herself and the door cracked so she could see outside.

Trouble stood outside in the shape of a fully armed Goblian. He was the same height as her, the same build and roughly the same shape. His skin was green. His nose was long and pointed and his clothes were rags. He was quick but not that quick. Widget got the door shut before he could push it open.

She locked the door and leant against the wood. She concentrated and wound her magic into the door so that the Goblian couldn't break through it.

"Wood now magic, you now have might,

Keep it out there, keep things right,

With word and whisper I do ask,

So please be diligent about your task."

The carpet was thick so she couldn't hear if the

Goblian was still there and she wasn't going to look through the keyhole. It was a well known Goblian trick to stick a sharp long thorn through the keyhole if they saw an eye there. That would blind whoever looked. Not that the puppet could be blinded but she didn't want to be damaged. Then she realised that there wasn't actually a keyhole anyway. The door unlocked with a plastic magnetic swipe card.

Now she was stuck. There were Goblians in the hotel and if they were hungry or mischievous then they would start causing damage or trouble. The other doors weren't protected and other people in the hotel were at risk.

Widget noticed something move and looked down. There was a note being pushed under the door. She smiled. "Oh come on, I know better than that. Of course I'm not going to touch it."

She picked up a hairbrush and pulled the note through from under the door and dragged it into the bathroom, over the lip of the shower tray and it lay in the shower looking intriguing. Now she had to do something about it.

Frixians have a failing, they are curious and that note was torment. So much so that she forgot about the Goblian at the door and had to use all her concentration to keep telling herself not to open and read the note. It screamed to her to be read.

There was nothing that she could think that it would be worth a Goblian writing to her. Indeed she didn't know that Goblians could read and write.

So whatever it was it was bad.

Widget searched the luggage in the vague hope that there was something useful there like a cricket bat. It wasn't anything that was likely to be there and even the stool in the room didn't look useful. As weapons went the room was pretty poorly armed. The woodwork was flimsy melamine and there wasn't anything there that looked useful.

It was bad. She was a lone Frixian trapped in a hotel room with a Goblian in the corridor and probably hundreds more downstairs.

Widget perched herself on the edge of the toilet and looked at the piece of paper as if an answer would leap out of it. Then she decided that staring at it wasn't probably healthy either. It was slightly grubby after being in the Goblian's pocket, slightly folded at the corners and it certainly looked as though the Goblian had carried it for a while.

She needed more excuses not to come to a decision to either flush the note, or read it. It was a difficult decision as it could have magic on it.

She sniffed it and there was the smell of magic so it

was obviously cursed.

There was a rattle at the door. She had forgotten about the Goblian but he had not forgotten about her. He was still there, still green, still nasty and still intent on killing her. She was still trapped in the hotel room and still on her own and still wondering what to do.

She thought about calling Stormcrow. It would be a long flight but she knew he would come. A flying goat would cause chaos and would put him in danger but it was an option. Then again he was locked in the shed back at the smallholding so he would have to break his way out. That would leave the other goats exposed as they wouldn't be safely locked in and he wouldn't be with them.

Stormcrow wasn't known for his subtlety so he would probably walk straight into the hotel as well. It would be amusing but would break the general rule of low profile.

She went to the window to see if she could get any ideas from there. The window was closed and it was a long way down to the ground. She thought about it. First of all she wished they had a room on the ground floor. Then she thought that one through and was glad that they were on a higher floor as Goblians don't climb well.

She cast a cautious look over her shoulder to make sure that the door was still in place. She was very afraid and really didn't know what to do. She could open the door and fight the Goblian but she would probably lose. He was stronger and better armed. She could leave the puppet body and run away but that would break the spell on the door, he would rip the puppet to pieces and would probably kill Angel and Niall when they came back. That was not the answer.

She had to think but the thought of the Goblian at the door really didn't help. Then she spotted the river, Goblians can't swim. That river was full of very deep water. So, she started planning around luring the Goblian out onto the water and drowning him. That was hard as Frixians can't swim either. Then she thought about it. She couldn't swim once but after being in the cave with the Weaver and her experience in the stream she now knew how. Now that was handy. Also, she was a cloth puppet, not a solid skin and bone thing like a Goblian. She was going to get soaked but the body itself would float. Magic would keep her dry, the same spell that she had created to be able to walk about at Pengraig without getting wet and muddy.

She had to make sure that the Goblian would sink. She looked around the room, looking for something that would help. It was a seemingly futile gesture but it was better than no gesture at all. She knew that even if he went out there he might not drown. She knew she had to weigh his pockets down.

The Goblian rattled the door again as if to remind her that he was still there. His voice hissing. "Open the door little Frixian. Make it easy on yourself or I will go and kill your little friends. They are crunchy and tasty and they will make this grumble in my belly go away."

Widget took a deep breath. She knew it was an awful situation. "No I won't. They are out in a public place. Someone would grab you and squish you and put you in a zoo or worse they would put you in a laboratory and dissect you to see how you work."

It went silent after she heard a little gasp. It was a minor victory but at that point she really needed the boost.

It didn't last long. The hissing voice was there again. "Open the door. Now. They aren't out there in a public place, they are down in the foyer playing backgammon with their friends."

The smile that had crept onto Widget's face soon faded. "No I won't and I won't read your note either. I'm not that stupid."

She heard the Goblian's foot stamp with a dull thud

on the carpet outside. It was followed by a thump as he kicked the door and an "ouch" because it hurt. "Open the door nasty Frixian."

She couldn't help laughing a little as she thought of the Goblian hopping in the corridor holding his foot. She needed a plan and she was starting to get one. She needed bricks or stones to heavy his bones and then words would certainly hurt him. She thought for a while and that infuriated the Goblian even more. He was about to kick the door again but thought better of it.

Widget went to the window and carefully opened it, quietly, so the Goblian didn't hear what she was doing. She then held out her hand and whispered "Stones of glory, stones most light, come and help me in my plight. Fly across the air so clear, make you far away stones come near."

Four medium sized stones rose up and floated across the river and landed on the carpet. They were dirty and wet and lay there, stone still.

She looked at them and smiled. "Stone so light I see you there, come and help me with some flare. Black and shiney, be all gold, be back to normal when you are told. Little stone that seems so light, become heavy when the time is right. Stay that way when I tell you true, now you know what you must do."

The stones sat on the carpet, shining and beautiful, burnished gold. They glistened and glimmered as she lifted them as they were very light and put them on the window sill. She then listened.

It was very quiet. The carpet was too soft to know what the Goblian was up to but as she could still smell him she knew he was there. He was quiet which was unusual for a Goblian. He was obviously confused as nothing had gone to plan.

Suddenly the Goblian lost patience, squealed in frustration, forgot and kicked the door. Then he squealed in pain. "Open the door. You are supposed to open it. I want you to open it. I told you to open it."

Widget sat on the bed for a moment cross legged to calm herself. She knew that if the Goblian could break in he would have done it by then. She also knew that the longer she waited the more frustrated the Goblian would get and the more likely he would be to really get things wrong for himself. She knew he wasn't going to go away either and when her friends came back he would hurt them if he didn't go downstairs and hurt them before then.

She knew she didn't have all night.

In her pocket she had her popping candy, safely sealed in a zip lock bag so that no Goblian could be attracted to it from a distance. She put a bit of it on the stones and on the window sill. She knew that their weakness for candy would help and when they eat it, it made them silly. She knew if it didn't she would be in trouble.

She looked out of the window and looked down, looking for how she was going to climb down. Then she slapped her forehead with her palm as she thought about it, she is a puppet.

She got on the window sill and then jumped. She stepped out of the puppet and let the toy fall. It was easy then to use her magic to let it float down gently and it landed elegantly in the grass outside the hotel.

She then stepped back into the body and began to whisper. "Little door you have done your job. You have the Goblian his success did rob. Now it is time to let him come in. As I know his patience is wearing thin."

As Widget ran away she heard the door splinter as the Goblian came crashing through the door. He saw the gold and forgot anything else as he also smelt and saw the popping candy. He eat the candy and picked up the stones and put them in his pocket for later. He was already on the window sill and after he had greedily devoured the candy he spotted Widget down on the grass below.

She used magic to throw some of the candy into the grass, rejoined her puppet body and ran off as the Goblian too jumped through the window so he could chase her. He screamed as he hit the ground, his limbs nearly snapping and he had really hurt himself. But anger kept him going until he passed the popping candy and had to stop. He eat it quickly which gave Widget the advantage. She ran, he ran, she ran faster, he ran faster. Then she got to the river and across it she had spotted a crane when they had driven in earlier. The river was large but she jumped in after whispering. "Magic spell please keep me dry. If I get wet I know I will cry. So keep me safe and keep me warm. From when I get in there until the dawn."

She jumped in and paddled like a dog as she couldn't really work out how to translate being a dragon with a tail to paddling with hands and feet.

There was a splash behind her and she smiled. "Nasty Goblian you must die. If you were good then I would try. Those rocks most magicked must now be true. Be heavy again and do what you do."

The Goblian wiggled and squiggled and paddled and splashed. He couldn't swim so no matter how much he splashed and splashed he still sunk like a stone to the bottom of the river when the stones became heavy in his pocket. He was gone, food for fishes.

Widget splashed herself slowly to the other side,

avoiding the ducks. She dragged herself out, bone dry, and sat on the bank. Then she smelt it again, Goblian. They were everywhere and they were closing in.

She ran to the crane which had been part of her plan and climbed up the metal skeletal frame until she was at the top. She could then see the Goblians all around, moving in. There were lots of them but they didn't think to look up and obviously hadn't seen her. They were looking down and around and in and out as they too could smell and they smelt Frixian. They soon got bored and wandered off.

When she didn't smell them anymore she went back to her room and went into the bathroom. She went to the mirror and brushed her hair, pulling her hair straight where it had come even more adrift and wishing she had a needle and thread.

The door was hanging off its hinges and very broken. She tried to put it back in place but it wouldn't stay there and nearly fell on her. She looked at it and frowned. "Now that is a problem. What am I going to do now? It is broken. Then it is only broken in this timeline. I need to take it back to a time when it isn't broken and then pull it into this timeline to leave it unbroken.

Little crystal do your stuff. This door is looking pretty rough. Bring it forwards and throw this back.

Make it better without even a crack."

She took a crystal out of her bag and touched it to the door and the door appeared unbroken again.

Somewhere in the past the cleaner was annoyed to find that guests had broken the door before leaving. She called the janitor who had the door replaced. The timeline was damaged but not in anyway that would cause any repercussions.

Next it was the note's turn. "Little note you are not wanted. You will not have your purpose granted. So up you float to flush away. I will not read you any day." The note floated into the air and landed in the toilet bowl. With a smile Widget flushed it away to a place where nobody could carelessly come upon it and want to read it.

She smiled to herself confident that she could be as curious as she liked as she would never know what was written on that piece of paper.

She closed the window and sat on the window sill for a while watching the family of ducks on the now moon drenched river. It was wonderfully normal. Everywhere in Cardiff people were doing mundane things in their wonderful mundane world. They were living their wonderful normal lives and out there some were sitting in bars talking while others did other things. They would be in restaurants eating interesting food, walking the streets enjoying the bright lights of Christmas. Goodwill to all men and peace on earth. A world that doesn't need Goblians. Corners should be dark without fear. Beds should only have dust bunnies under them and cupboards are for clothes.

She smiled as she thought about more of her kind coming to the world. It was a happy thought. There was a new control box and they knew where the portal was. She couldn't wait to get home now and get on with it all.

She then smiled, climbed back into her basket and waited for her friends to come back. Then she got bored, stepped out of her body and went to look for them.

The Goblian had lied. They weren't playing backgammon they were out and about around Cardiff Bay looking for something to eat.

The Bay teemed with life. Office Parties and Saturday night revellers were enjoying the atmosphere. The good restaurants were lively and packed, some others were empty for one reason or the other. There was choice and bustle and she was invisible, invisible was good.

She was enjoying the decorations on the Bay and came to a little gingerbread cottage. Those things always gave her the creeps as they were often occupied by old crones who eat children. Why else would you make your house out of food? It wasn't, it was a decoration. But inside she did see something, a tiny elf, a real one. He was sitting amongst the decorations and enjoying being ignored by everyone. She smiled and waved. He was cautious but waved back when nobody was looking.

Then she spotted her three friends who were hunting the bay for a good restaurant and by the look on Niall's face it wasn't going well.

After the day she had had knowing they were safe was good. She left them there and went back to her basket to think about the day's happenings and to get ready for getting back home and her next adventure.

4 THE TOYMAKER'S DREAM

The rain hammered down relentlessly on the dirty pavements on a dirty street in a dirty part of town. The houses and flats were shabby. They were crammed together for maximum income for minimum investment. Houses had been cut apart to make the maximum number of flats and many of them were so small that there was hardly room to move in them once the occupants had a bed and a sofa. The wonders of bedsit land.

In one of those bedsits an old man pushed his hands down on the arm of his threadbare winged back chair in front of his two bar electric fire and stood up. He grabbed his walking stick with his gnarled arthritic hand and used it to help himself to get up the rest of the way.

He looked around his room. Every chair and shelf

was stuffed full of his memories. The ornaments and photographs were all dusty, tired and old as he could not manage to keep them as he once had. Then he had once lived in a big house and had a lovely little shop where all the people came to see what he sold. He had never been alone then. Maggie had been with him then. But Maggie had died. Her chair was still there, he had brought that with him even though she would never sit in it again. His beautiful Maggie. His amazing and kind Maggie. She was gone and he was alone. Their child was far away too. Their beautiful boy Archie had been gone some thirty years too. Thirty years to the day since a drunk driver had run him over and in that moment he had been gone from the world.

The shop had been everything to them after that day. The shop had been full of wonderful children and wonderful parents buying wonderful toys for happy times. He had felt the loss of his own child but the love of the children, that had made up for it a bit.

His hands were gnarled now and arthritic. He couldn't make toys anymore. Then again the children didn't want them now anyway. They wanted computers, phones and other things like that. They had no place for puppets, dolls, teddies and wooden trains. They had no room for toys which encouraged the imagination. His toys had often been imaginary friends or real ones. They had no room for that in the consumer packaged rush towards the developing technological age.

Then his Maggie had got sick and he needed to look after her. So he sold the shop, he sold his house and he spent the last of her days caring for her.

He forgot his toys, he forgot his shop, he forgot. Not today, today he remembered and it made him sad.

His chest felt tight, he felt sick and dizzy but he had no tea and tea was what he wanted. A good cup of tea. He had had no tea for days now but today he wanted tea. It was Christmas Eve and he knew if he didn't get tea today he could not have tea tomorrow. Not that he couldn't do without tea tomorrow but he wanted the option to have a cup of tea on Christmas morning. Not that Christmas meant much to him.

He had received his usual expensive printed card from his brother and sister in law. It was as always impersonally printed with their name and address as well rather than a personal message. He always smiled, the address lest he forgot to send them a card to add to their huge stack of appreciation which would deck their happy halls.

As he sat down to his microwaveable TV turkey dinner and Christmas Pudding for one he would be able to think back down the years. He knew he would be thinking of Maggie and what it was like when she had been alive. There would be a huge plump bird perfectly cooked and steaming invitingly. The room was filled with its aroma every year in the way that only a roast dinner can do. He remembered how they had danced together one year to the amusement of their little boy.

How he had laughed as they had waltzed crazily around the table to land exhausted in their chairs before raising a glass of champagne to the joy of the season.

His glass was empty now, if he actually had a glass, he couldn't remember.

There was nothing to toast anyway.

He remembered the months running up to Christmas where he sewed, glued and stuck toys together. Those long days and longer nights of no sleep. He worked so that Santa's sack was full and his elves could deliver the toys on Christmas morning to children who had been good and perhaps a little bad as all children are want to be.

He smiled as he thought of the wooden goat rocking horse, rocking goat, he had made one year. It had been made specifically for a lovely little girl who loved goats. He wished he could have seen her bright face on Christmas morning after Santa had delivered it.

They were all ghosts in the ether now, all memories. The television in the corner was now blank and dead. It had broken sometime in November and with his pension being so small he didn't have the money to have it fixed or get another one, even second hand. He missed the sound of the Christmas programs though, even though he had seen them many times.

He shuffled slowly across the room and picked up his threadbare old coat from the hook on the back of the door. While balancing with a stick in one hand he put one arm through it, swapped hands and put the other arm through it and pulled the coat on. His painful joints made every action a chore. He was old now, eighty at the last birthday. A birthday he had spent alone, his company was the cards so thoughtfully printed and sent by his family via Moonpig or some other such internet card manufacturer, probably prompted by a calendar reminder rather than actually remembering him. The card was delivered promptly on the day so that it could bring some brightness to his lonely hours.

He had sat near the phone that day. He even moved his old wooden chair to the small table where the phone sat so he wouldn't miss a call. No calls came. He had his cards, their duty was done. They were still on his dresser, he hadn't put them away yet even though his birthday had been in October.

He put his old flat cap on his mostly bald head and wrapped his old knitted scarf around his gnarly old neck. He smiled as he remembered the click, click, click of the knitting needles as Maggie had knitted it. She had always sat in that very same chair, looking up occasionally to smile at him.

The scarf was still keeping him warm although much else he had had was now gone. It was memories and physical protection from the storm that was out there.

He opened the old door, its paint peeling off and he stepped out into the dusty corridor. His old shoes made no sound on the threadbare carpet as he shuffled to the stairs.

He gripped the handrail with all of his strength and for a moment he almost gave up and went home. He used his stick and then tortoise like he crept down the stairs one by one. Foot before foot, his hand slipping to grip again.

At the bottom of the stairs the vast expanse of the hallway seemed an impossible hurdle. There was nothing to hold onto and the tiles were slippery under his stick where other neighbours had brought water inside dripping from coats and umbrellas.

He put a cautious foot on the floor and put weight on it. Then another foot was put down off of the stairs and then he shuffled without raising his feet across the quarry tiles to the old glass panelled front door.

The hand that gripped the door knob wasn't the hand he wanted to see. That hand was old, he wanted to see his younger hands. It was liver spotted and paper fragile. Those gnarly knuckles would never make toys again. He sighed looking at the single piece of tinsel hanging over a wooden framed mirror by the door. That was something that made him smile. Christmas decorations for himself and the five other people who had taken rooms in the building. He had found it in his cupboard and brought hit down to share with the others. He didn't know the others, he had vaguely passed them and been ignored on the stairs. He didn't even know who lived there. He almost smiled as he tucked his scarf into his coat, pulled his collar up against the cold, opened the door and stepped out onto the empty street.

Cars lined the road as those who drove them were not at work today as it was Sunday. There were a few gaps left by those who had gone shopping. He didn't know who they belonged to. Like everyone else he kept himself to himself and that was how people liked it. He longed to speak to them. He had tried but all he got was a polite "good morning" and they went on with their busy lives.

He passed the gates which led to the doors where some had hung wreaths for Christmas. They made him smile but they made him sad too. Wreaths reminded him that people died, many at Christmas. He couldn't see how wreaths could be happy. There were so many people he had once known who were now gone. The children he had made toys for, even they were grown now and didn't need him anymore. That was sad he thought but that was the way of life. Life was for the young.

He shuffled down the road slowly, his stick tapping on the wet pavement as the rain hammered down on him. He had no umbrella, that had broken long ago and he had had to throw it away. His hands weren't strong enough to hold it up anyway as the wind dashed the rain against him. He could feel it biting his face, running down his neck and soaking him. It pushed through the fibres of his coat, making it wet and as he walked he could feel the moisture soaking through his clothes underneath his coat. He shuffled on, he wanted his tea. That was the most important thing to him now. That moment of happiness on Christmas morning.

He got to the shop and the bright lights inside sparkled as the Christmas decorations reminded him that life goes on. The family sized boxes of biscuits that had been stacked before Christmas were now gone, sold to those who would be sitting having them with their tea. They had their biscuits and their family. He looked at a small pack of biscuits and reached into his pocket. He pulled out his half moon leather wallet and opened it up. He slid the change out into the cup made by the lid and he counted the money he had. He had enough for a small box of tea but not enough for biscuits. No biscuits for him today. Then biscuits were for when people called by so they could be put neatly on a saucer and offered to guests. Nobody would be calling on him, so he didn't need biscuits.

He picked up a very small pack of value tea and took it to the counter. He had gone to that counter a hundred times at least but still the shop keeper merely smiled, took his money and the "kerchiiinnng" of the till was his friendly greeting.

"Good afternoon Mr Jones".

Frederick smiled. "Good afternoon Mr Patel. Have you had a good day?"

Mr Patel looked up a little stunned at the extra conversation. "Yes thank you Mr Jones. Yourself?"

Frederick thought about his day where he had sat alone in his chair and thought about absent friends. He thought about his Christmas Day to come but he knew that the question was purely a polite one, spoken with no real interest in the actual answer although he would dearly have loved to have heard about Mr Patel's day. His eyes were watering slightly. "Yes thank you Mr Patel."

He then took his tea and shuffled to the door. He pulled the door and the bell rang as he stepped out into the rainy street and shuffled back to his bedsit.

He climbed the stairs carefully and slowly and opened his door. As he stepped inside he pulled off his wet coat which was dripping a puddle on the floor. He pulled off his scarf and squeezed the water out of it. He squeezed the water out of his flat cap and went to the fire. He was cold, beyond cold. He needed to dry himself off and his clothes were soaked to his underwear so he hoped to dry them too. He didn't have others.

He put his finger on the switch in anticipation of the waft of warmth that would come from the bar. He pushed it. Nothing happened.

His jaw dropped in horror as he shuffled to his lamp. He touched the switch and with awful dread he realised that the lamp didn't work either.

He went to his coat then remembered there were no more coins in his wallet that would make that fire light again. His power had run out and the coin meter had ticked its last turn around. Tonight his light would bring no golden glow to his sparsely furnished room. He would have to make do with a single candle, the only one he had left from the glorious silver candlestick that had graced their twenty foot dining table in time gone by.

He went to the bathroom and grabbed his shabby threadbare towel and began to dry himself off as he shivered uncontrollably. Dry, dry, dry, he knew it was going to be important as tonight there would be no warm fire to sit beside.

Frederick Jones pulled the thin duvet up over himself. It afforded little comfort as the biting chill of the room nibbled at his old bones. He grasped an old book in his hands as the single candle offered him a little heat and a little light.

He turned the pages one by one, looking at the pictures and the designs. His old toymaking journal was all that he had left of his old life. He hadn't looked at it for years but tonight it brought him comfort. His little stories were scribbled around each of the toy designs. Every toy had its past and present, its own little story of how it had come to be and what had happened to it.

He picked up his old pencil, half the length it used to be. He sharpened it again and again to write more and every scrap of it had been used over the years. It was sharp, he had sharpened it the last time he had written something. He began reading what he had last written. It wasn't at the end of the book, there were still a few pages left. His handwriting was now a shaky travesty of his neat Copperplate script of earlier years. There were crossings out where before he could have written good and true without having to change anything. The words were just about readable.

Firelight, candles, mince pies alright

Are what is needed on just such a night

When toys are completed

And to Santa they are sent

To be given to children

With a good intent

Holly and Ivy

Yule log it is lit

No time for depression

Well perhaps just a bit

As toys now are different

No imagination they do need

And a bright sparkly mind

Their ownership to feed

Wooden trains lay unpainted

Trapped in the box

Cuddly toys lay unwanted

Along with wood blocks

They have no batteries and circuits

No shiny buttons to press

So who really cares now

For a doll's pretty dress.

He was looking at this page in his book as he fell asleep.

Shadows lengthened in the woodland as a unicorn and her mate danced around each other. White flowing manes blowing in the gentle breeze, hooves dancing and muscles rippling. They danced and circled on the edge of a seemingly endless lake.

In the sky birds were singing and the crickets played their chirrupy song to add to the chorus of nature.

The sun shone down brightly on the greens and subtle hues of nature. Willow trees draped their branches into the water and a black swan floated gracefully past, her noble head looking around as her mate swam effortlessly across the lake to join her.

Frederick Jones was standing in the clearing feeling confused. He looked down at his feet. His shoes shone black and shiny, as well polished as he had ever made them. His suit was impeccable, as it had always been. His cravat was neatly tied with a single diamond pin sparkling in the sunlight. He remembered the day he had had to sell it to pay for medicine. His walking stick was now his old elegant walking cane he had owned in his youth which slipped effortlessly between the fingers of his calf skin gloves.

He straightened himself up. He cast off the shadow of his arthritic stance and bent double gait that he had endured for so long and walked a few steps without pain.

In his mind he knew he was dreaming but he didn't care. He wanted to be here, a place he had often escaped to when things got rough. This was where his toys lived, truly lived, where their stories started and ended. It was his safe place far from the greys and browns of the modern world.

This was a place where Maggie was no longer dead. She would be there in their beautiful cottage baking cookies and cleaning their home until it sparkled.

Their son would be there too, playing in the garden, an eternal blonde haired child who would never grow up. Their old grey and white dog was there too. He had everything in his dream that he had lost in his life and in his dreams he was free. This was his world, the world where his toys were real.

There they were as if on cue. One by one they marched into the clearing. The wooden toy soldiers started the parade. Their immaculate red and black uniforms painted all the same. Their guns were held aloft over their shoulders and their boots hammering out the march that those behind followed.

Behind them came the wooden trains. The engines pulling carriages with other toys sitting in them. Bears, dolls and stuffed monkeys waved their hands and smiled at him.

Behind them came the rocking horses, rocking along as part of the parade.

He remembered each one of them. Each stroke of the saw, each sweep of the brush. Loving care was what made his toys so special, or rather was what had made them. They weren't the sort of toys that were wanted now.

A single tear ran down his face as he felt a hand on his shoulder. He turned to see a beautiful black haired woman dressed in white who was standing behind him. Her skin was the finest porcelain, it was as if her features were painted on though they were very real. She reached out a finger and swept the tear from his face.

He jumped slightly as he had not realised she was there. "Frederick Jones, you have made some beautiful toys and you have made so many people happy. You may have a wish."

Frederick looked at her in disbelief. "You haven't been here before. What are you doing in my dream? I didn't dream you."

The woman smiled, her cat like slit pupils surprised him, her eyes were bright and sparkling. "You are dreaming me. This is a dream but this is also part of my world. So, you may have one wish and I mean it. Be careful what you ask for as it is in my power to grant it." She held her breath as she knew what she wanted him to ask and it was one moment that could change everything.

The old man now young looked down at his body which was now straight and strong. He pulled off his gloves and looked at his hands. They were young again. He felt his skin, no longer paper fragile. He looked around the dream world that he believed he had created in his mind. "Who are you? It is appropriate to ask to whom one is speaking when one is offered a wish such as you are offering."

The woman smiled. "Quite right, quite right. I am the Weaver of Dreams and I offer you one wish. Take it quickly for they do disappear if they are not claimed." The suspense was intense as she knew that she could not lead his wish.

Frederick thought about it. He could feel the chill in his bones and he knew it was from his living body. He felt the hopelessness so acutely that it sent an emotional shiver through his whole consciousness. He felt the loneliness of his bedsit and the uselessness of his life.

The woman took his hand and he felt himself spinning. Light flashed around him and he smelt roses, followed by lavender, followed by the soft loamy smell of damp woodland. Then he stopped moving. It was dark until he realised that he had shut his eyes. He opened them again.

He was in a small room. The room was wallpapered with a bright pattern which came alive with soldiers playing drums and other musical instruments. They were only a pattern on paper but they made the nursery bright and cheerful.

In the middle of the room there was a cot, in the cot was a baby and across the room was a chair full of toys. He had made those toys.

He smiled as he saw them and as he watched the child

woke up and was a baby no more. The child was about four and reached out for the toys but she could not reach them. He took one from the chair, a large brown bear which growled when it moved and he gave it to her. She settled down with the large brown bear and fell asleep.

The Weaver of Dreams smiled. "That she can sleep means that she can dream. That she can dream means that in the future she will still have those dreams as memories. She will remember you, you will see her again if you make the right choices now. Those dreams she will dream on nights like this will make her who she will be. So that small act has made a big difference already. Do you understand what I am trying to show you?

You are now in a world very different to how you imagine it as it is the world of true dreams. It is in parallel to your own. What happens here can have an effect on your world but it is also separate. So there are some rules. Come with me now and I will show you some things. Then you can make your wish."

He took her offered hand and they span through time as he saw world history playing out in reverse. He saw London through the years, he saw Manchester, Birmingham and all the other cities. He saw the world from space and then when the journey was finished he was standing in a room. The room was his, or had been. He recognised it as he was back in his toymaking workshop.

All around there were bits and pieces, just as he remembered it. Toys were half made, pensively waiting. His finished toys were on his finished shelf drying and waiting for collection or to be put into the shop if they weren't commissions. There was another shelf of toys waiting for other things to be done to them.

His younger self sat there, head in hands, asleep. He was half way through stuffing a cuddly monkey. He snored loudly, his head falling off of his hands and he was awake again. Awake and making toys. Sewing and sewing.

The scene sped up as the toys were finished and waiting. Maggie came in with a cup of tea for him. She took an interest in all the toys he had made as she always did. It was a fleeting moment as time sped on. He reached for Maggie as she passed by him but the Weaver caught his wrist. "I am sorry Frederick, you can't touch this scene as you were there and it is the past for you. You have lived through this timeline so you can't be in it again."

Frederick looked sad but his eyes keenly watched as the toys were made one by one.

The Dreamweaver put a hand on his shoulder. "It is time to move on. I have other things to show you and there is not very long for me to do this. There are things I am not allowed to tell you but remember what you have seen. Come with me again now, we must move on." She held her hand out.

Frederick took her hand again and they moved on. He was again in a shop, his shop but it was much later. The shelves were well stocked with beautiful toys but many were now not hand made and came in boxes. Colour filled the place, all manner of colours. It was bright and happy but at the same time it was tasteful. A huge Christmas tree was decorated in the corner. Small toys and bears hung on it as decorations, their price tags fluttering in the gentle breeze as the shop door opened and an elegant woman wearing blue with a matching blue jacket and a black fake fur coat walked in. She carried a large black handbag and a smile on her face.

She walked to the counter and looked around the shelves. "I am looking for a doll for my daughter. Can you make me something special?"

The young Frederick smiled. "Of course I can. Should it be a large or a small doll. Should it have a dress of green, blue or lilac? Should she have blonde hair, brown or red? Should she have freckles or no freckles?"

The woman smiled. "She should be three feet tall and I will leave it to you to choose the rest. When will she be ready? I would like her for my daughter's birthday next Wednesday. I know that it is Christmas on Thursday and you are probably rushed off your feet but please could you try?"

Frederick looked in his notebook which was stuffed with notes, stories and annotations. "I will have her ready for you on Tuesday."

The woman smiled and placed some notes on the table. "I hope this will be enough for a deposit."

The Toymaker smiled. "Indeed it will be. I don't usually ask for one but I am grateful for it. I will have her ready for you."

Frederick the elder looked at the Weaver of Dreams. "I remember this customer and the doll. I made it with the love and care I usually use to make a doll but that doll did feel special. I don't know why. I had to work night and day but I got it finished for her."

The Weaver smiled. "I know you did. Do you want to come and see what happened to the doll?"

Frederick smiled. "I would very much like to see that."

The world spun again and the scene changed. They

stood in a medium sized bedroom. The wallpaper was striped brown with brown floral bouquets in baskets between the parallel lines. The carpet was a thick blue and there was a bed in the corner opposite a couple of wardrobes either side of a fireplace painted white. The door was closed and the curtains were open.

He looked out of the window.

The garden was neatly set out. An immaculate rectangular lawn was mown to stripes. It was edged with a glorious array of border plants which were all in neat lines. White Alyssum edged the neat lawn. The next line was the gold of Marigold and then a riot of colour made up of many other plants.

To the right was a path lined on one side with dahlias and on the other chrysanthemums. It was a truly fairytale paradise of colour, shape and form. Three apple trees were heavily laden with fruit and there were hanging lights for the night time.

Two young girls were sitting on the floor playing with their toys. They were playing with plastic horses and dolls in beautiful ball gowns. They both had their own houses set up for their dolls and were making up stories for them. Wild adventures and ordinary days filled those dolls' lives.

One was blonde, the other dark haired. The blonde

had a huge house for her dolls, the dark was content with a smaller area.

Plastic doll sized wardrobes made up the walls along with bits of cardboard. Tiny hangers held spare dresses and each doll had a pet dog.

The dark haired girl had plaits and a cheeky smile. The blonde was short haired. Her eyes looked around everything as they made up their stories. The princess and the goosegirl. One wanted to be a princess and the other the goose girl. One wanted the castle, the other didn't.

The dark haired girl got up and left the room and when she was gone her playmate reached over and broke the ears off of one of her horses, pushing it over so that it looked as if the ears had snapped off.

The Toymaker looked in horror as he saw time played out at speed and out of time. Over the months toys disappeared and some broke and the brown haired girl wondered where things were going.

The Toymaker was angry and as he looked at the Dream Weaver he saw that she was angry too. "I use my wish. I want to use my doll to protect that little girl."

The Weaver smiled. Then you shall bind the first Frixian into a toy. This is how it started, all those years ago. You can take the bodyless and hopeless spirit that can't help the world and bind it into that toy. That is your gift, your wish is granted."

The Toymaker reached out and touched the toy he had made. He felt the spirit that had watched over the little girl and he allowed it to become part of the doll temporarily.

The blonde haired girl was on her own in the room when the doll got up. The girl was no longer in the room after the doll had walked across the room and reached out for her. She was on her way down the stairs screaming that the doll had moved.

The Weaver moved time on and again the doll did the same thing, again and again until the girl stopped breaking and taking the toys.

The scene shifted again and the Toymaker sat in what had been his shop. He sat at the cash desk while his younger incarnation was asleep after a long time making Christmas toys as he did when it was coming up to Christmas, he lived in the workshop. He looked around all the toys. "Wouldn't it be wonderful if these toys could protect children, if they could move and be all those things that children imagine them to be?"

The Weaver smiled. "I will give you the rest of your wish as you have said that. Is that your wish?"

The Toymaker didn't need to think about it. He nodded. "Yes, that is my wish."

The Weaver grinned widely. "I had hoped you would say that. From this day on and for all time you will be The Toymaker. But, there is a price to be paid. You cannot return to your body as your body is dieing. I am offering you another option.

There are aliens living on this planet who are living without form and unable to do anything against the injustices they see. They wander the ether unable to touch anything and the are sad. They have seen the bad things in this world and they want to help. I would like you to help them. I want you to become The Toymaker who binds them into toys so that they can look after children. As it is your wish, I can offer you this. Do you accept?"

The Toymaker smiled. His old face lit up with a light that had not been seen on his tired old face for years. His wrinkles were deep, his eyes were watery and old, his hand were gnarled and arthritic. He looked down at them as he sat in his chair and then looked at the Weaver. "How can I do such a thing? My hands would not make toys now. My toys are not wanted anymore."

The Weaver smiled. "I have already told you, it will not be with that body. You are right, those hands will never again make toys. Those eyes will never again see the beautiful toys that you have made. For tonight you will die. You will pass to dust and that will be the end of Frederick Jones. He will be a memory. I will show you some more before you have a final chance to accept or decline my offer. I will give you one more chance to see before you decide as once chosen there is no going back." She held out her hand.

Frederick took the impossibly fragile hand in his and the world spun around again. Time had moved on and when the mist that swirled around them cleared he saw he was at a graveside. The minister was there with his book but there was nobody else there. The minister said the words. The minister picked up soil and threw it onto the coffin and as the dirt hit the box Frederick looked down at the engraved plate. "Frederick Jones, Died 25th December 2015"

The sight chilled him to the bone. He looked at the coffin and he knew it was real. The scene changed and he was in his bedsit, standing beside his old battered chair. It was empty now. His notebook was on the table and a burnt down candle in a cheap metal candlestick stood beside it.

He saw a man in the room and vaguely recognised him as it had been so many years since he had last seen his brother. He did recognise the voice which came from behind him and he turned to see his sister in law who had been going through his things.

She had a cardboard box on the table but there was nothing in it. She was looking through drawers and the wardrobe and she shook her head. "Nothing of any value here. The old coot didn't have a stock of gold hidden anywhere. The silly old fool must have spent the lot. Not even an old toy that might be a collector's item that we can put on Ebay. Nothing but fifteen pence in his silly little wallet." She took the leather wallet out of her pocket and flipped it into the box. "What should we do with all this rubbish?"

His brother in law looked around the room. "I don't know. House clearance is expensive so I suppose we will have to do it ourselves. Did you bring the bin bags I put out? I forgot them."

The woman went to her coat which was hung on the back of his door. "Yes, even the bags are going to cost us money. Oh well, lets get on with it.

We don't want any more rent to come out of his estate."

The brother in law nearly choked. "What estate? Are you expecting some sort of will reading? I've seen the Will. He had nothing left at all. Absolutely nothing. What you see here is what you get. A load of old rubbish. That was all he had. Come on, he died of a chill because he didn't have the money for the meter so he had no heating. The stupid old buzzard went out to buy a packet of tea and got himself wet. The post mortem said that he died as he went to bed and the duvet was damp as well. He died in is sleep."

The woman shrugged. Then she looked at the kitchen area, picked up the packet of tea and put it in the cardboard box. Her husband glared at her but she shrugged. "Waste not want not. Didn't he have a pension or something? Perhaps a life insurance policy?"

The brother in law sighed. "Sadly not. I can't imagine he would have paid into anything like that. He didn't really have a grip on the world at all. He made toys until his hands were too bad and then his wife got sick and he sold the lot to make sure she had every medication she needed. Bit of a sad story really. I'd been meaning to visit him but you know how busy I am. I had to admit that I did keep putting it off."

The woman smiled. "Oh well, better that he is out of his misery then."

She walked over to the table and picked up The Toymaker's book. "What about this? Do you think this would be worth something? We could try it on Ebay?"

Frederick looked at the Weaver. His eyes were full of tears. "That journal was my life."

The Weaver smiled. "Don't worry, Widget will bid on it and I'll make sure nobody else does. We'll get it for you."

Frederick wiped his eyes with his sleeve. "Who is Widget?"

The Weaver thought for a moment. "Do you accept that you will be The Toymaker? That is a job you will have forever and you don't get paid. If you choose to take it then you will forsake your mortal body. There is no going back as you will technically die tonight. You will then be a spirit and as a spirit you can bind Frixians into toys. If we can find a suitable puppet for you then for comfort and to fit in with the others I'll get one for you. You are of course invited to move in with Widget and the others. You will forever be able to bind Frixians into their chosen material body.

Widget and Gadget are two such aliens. They were bound into their bodies a long time ago. Frixians can leave the bodies at will and return once they are bound. They write books but they also fight the evil Goblians.

They have a battle on their hands as the wicked Goblians are also aliens from another planet and they are here too. They harm children as they feed on the energy they get from making them angry, depressed and spiteful. They like nothing better than the children's creativity and better part of their nature not to develop.

Widget and Gadget have to open a gateway so that Frixian spirits can pass through. Once you can bind them then the numbers of useful Frixians on this planet can increase.

Your lifetime of making puppets and toys has made you an unique spirit. You have brought so much happiness to so many by what you have done that the magic created by this happiness is bound to you. I can offer you this because of who you are and what you have done. So I ask you again, last chance to back out, do you accept?"

The old man laughed. "You mean you are offering a toymaker the opportunity to spend eternity with toys making people happy and keeping them safe? Do you think I seriously have a choice? Of course I accept. So what happens next?"

The Weaver smiled and the scenery changed. They were standing in a cave and the old man was faced with a huge red dragon. The dragon reached out a claw and touched the old man. The man's body evaporated into smoke. The smoke drifted through the ether and its sinuous tendrils percolated through the keyhole of a farmhouse in Mid Wales. The tendrils touched something soft, something miraculous, something new. The tendrils took the shape of the puppet, one he knew he was only borrowing while his long term body was found.

The tendrils took the shape of the puppet which sat lifeless beside Widget.

The puppet took on life and form.

The puppet looked up and moved. His spiky blonde fur hair was a crazy contrast to the black curly wig that Widget had chosen. His face was more pointed, his nose a simple pink ball. He had been made by a different company. The puppet was a standard off the peg item which had a black and blue shirt which looked like a football shirt and denim trousers which were patched decoratively.

He lifted his new hands and his new eyes looked at them. He looked around the little area under the stairs and he looked through the grid of the fire guard at the room the other side of it. This was the first time he saw the living room at Pengraig. He marveled at the engraved mirror which took up one wall and the old cabinets. He didn't like the mud on the floor but when he saw the dogs he knew why it was there. He sat very very still when the dog saw him. It wagged its tail, picked up a bone which looked ominous and trotted over, had a sniff then trotted off, taking the bone.

The puppet next to him, Widget, turned her head to look at him. Her triangular nose sniffed the air. "Welcome. You are real. That is good but you aren't Frixian. Who are you?"

Frederick couldn't remember his name. All he could remember was that he was The Toymaker. "I don't know. I think I am The Toymaker."

Widget smiled. "Well, that was easy. I suppose that the Weaver of

Dreams sent you. Welcome to our home and to our family. This is Gadget."

Gadget bowed her head. "She lives here too. We'll take you and show you our time and space travelling device later. This is very exciting. Where did you come from?"

Gadget smiled. "Yes, you are welcome. It will take you some time to get used to being in that body. It feels odd for a while but you do have to remember the rules. You can only move when there are no humans in the room. That is a fact, you can't break that. Then you aren't a Frixian so you might be able to. You will have to try that one out later. Try to be on a chair or near somewhere comfortable if a human is likely to walk in on you or your puppet will be a mess very quickly and we don't wash. Don't let the dogs get hold of you. I have seen what they do to their toys and they probably wouldn't know the difference. Well other than Jack, he is a fey creature anyway.

You probably won't be able to speak in this world either. Do you know that?"

The Toymaker shook his head. "I don't know anything. I said yes to becoming the Toymaker and here I am. No guide book I'm afraid."

Widget smiled kindly. "It will be a bit of a shock but even though you probably can't speak you can form a telepathic link to Angel. If other people are around you can guide their conversation the way you want it or you can do a conversation with Angel where she states your question before part answering it or offering it to others. That way you can almost speak.

The Toymaker took in a deep breath and let it out slowly. It was a spiritual breath and unnecessary but it made him feel better. "Alright, now I think I have it straight in my head. I have died and my spirit has been put into this puppet so that I can help you to bind Frixians to puppets and toys." The Toymaker looked worried. "So what do we do now?"

Widget looked down at her hands. It was a habit that was becoming more and more common as it was the natural position for the puppet. "Well now we have to go to the Secret Garden and open up the Gateway. It is only temporary but it has to be done. The TAVERN isn't sorted out as yet. The controls haven't been configured. We went to Cardiff to borrow the Tardis to get the moon rock on the right day and left that to be made into the key. I spent a long time out of time on the Tardis using bits and pieces from their store room to make a control box but as mentioned it isn't configured and Elir is working on it. All we have to do now is solve the problem of the key.

We also need to send a message to our future selves."

The Toymaker frowned. "I can see that would be a problem although I have no idea what you are talking about. I'll just nod my head and listen and learn if you don't mind. I will pretend that I know what this is all about in the hope that it isn't a dream. It has been a busy day, the day I died."

Widget was thoughtful. "Also, we don't have bodies for the Frixians we can get here yet either. Angel has found a company who can provide some of the bodies. She tried to tell them about what we are doing and to get them on board with helping but they didn't answer her. Once the spirits arrive they will need to go somewhere. We need the sprits to go there too. A lot to do."

The Toymaker thought about it. "You are writing all this as a novel aren't you? Well if you write in the novel that you need your future selves to know about this and the book is published it will be there for them in the future to read about it and know what they have to do, so they can do it."

Widget laughed. "You know for a newbie you have really grasped this well. I didn't think about that. Do you write? I saw your journal, it was full of wonderful stories about your toys. Would you like to write in the books?"

The Toymaker looked down at his cloth hands. "I am not sure how much good these hands will be. They need a human hand in them to make them work. They are gloves for the puppeteer unlike your hands which are stuffed already. They are floppy, useless."

Widget looked at him and looked at them. "You are quite right and those hands aren't going to be as useful. We will have to get you a different body."

Widget went to the laptop and logged into Angel's Ebay account. She put "puppet" in the search box and hit search. The Toymaker walked over to look. He was a bit wobbly on his feet and Gadget steadied him. There were quite a few on the list but one in particular caught their attention. It was a string puppet, an old fashioned one, about a foot and a half tall and it looked like Geppetto from the story of a puppet who wanted to be real. It was perfect in her mind. "Do you like that one?"

The Toymaker was beaming. "It is perfect. It looks like I used to look.

So we are going to buy it?"

Widget turned away from the keyboard. Well, hopefully. I have put in a bid which is the asking price and a little more. We will have to watch it and if someone else bids we'll have to bid some more. Angel won't mind I am sure.

You see this box, this is where you can write your stories. You don't need a pencil as you'd only have to type it up afterwards. You can type directly onto what is called a template and then publish. We will include one of your stories in our next book."

The Toymaker looked thoughtful. "I really wish I had my notes. The

Weaver said that if it went on Ebay she would ask Angel to buy it." Widget looked into Angel's "Purchase History". "Is this it?"

The Toymaker beamed as he saw a very badly photographed copy of his book. Hmm, should I be insulted that she only paid 99p for it?"

Gadget was thinking. "Do we have to go on calling

you The Toymaker?

Do you have a name?"

The Toymaker thought about it. "I can't remember my human name and that life is gone now."

Widget looked sad. "You had a life as a human, those memories must be wonderful."

The Toymaker smiled. "I was human. I was a man with a wife and a child. Both are dead now. Then again so am I now. I wish I'd met you all earlier, perhaps they could have been offered the opportunity to be puppet helpers too."

Widget shook her head. "That would not be possible. You are a one of a kind. It is not possible to put the souls of the dead into puppets. When a spirit dies it has a path to follow and it cannot be taken from that path. You had spent your life making toys and the Toymaker has always existed. You connected with that energy so your soul had a choice. It will never happen again and has never happened before. We would all love to bring back lost loved ones and we would all love more moments with them but we have to accept that unless the spirit wants to and there is a reason for it that is beyond us they have moved on. Memories are all we have and all that we are is a part of them."

Gadget sighed. "That is deep."

Widget laughed. "I'm not shallow but I understand things. We miss people don't we? I know we were hatched from eggs but do we love our parents any less? They are gone too."

The Toymaker thought about it. "I am the Toymaker forever but I would like another name, rather than just a job title. How did you get your names?"

Widget smiled. "A widget is a little plastic thing in a beer can. Gadget is something that does something. You should have a name that sort of fits what you do. Did you sew? I know it isn't technically correct as you don't make suits but how about Tailor?"

The Toymaker smiled. "I like the name Tailor, that shall be my name. I like that puppet, that shall be my body I hope."

Gadget looked thoughtful. "Well we can allocate you a goat as well. We all go goat riding at night when the weather is good. You can choose one yourself, they are all great. You will meet them later. There is Frixie Pfriend, she isn't a goat but she looks like a goat most of the time. There is Stormcrow, he is a beautiful big male with impressive horns, he is Widget's goat to ride. I like them all but Brenin, the Arapawa is my favourite and I ride him."

The Toymaker was thinking about it. "When my proper body arrives I will enjoy that. Can all goats fly?"

Gadget shook her head. "Goats fly because we give them the ability to do it. It only works on the males though. That is the way of it."

The Toymaker smiled. "My life here is going to be interesting. I am expected to write and ride goats, different I suppose. That sounds like fun." Widget looked sad. "Tailor, what is the problem?"

Tailor smiled and wiped away his tears. "I spent so many years alone and unwanted, feeling I was washed up and useless. This is a huge change.

Overnight I have a new home and new friends."

Widget looked bemused. "Why were you alone? Did you lose your family?"

Tailor took a deep breath. "I had family but they had their own interests and life so they didn't have time for me. They never forgot to send me a card on my birthday or Christmas though so I was better off than some.

I used to go to a Centre where people like me could get together. It was bright and happy and there was tea. That was a good time. There were free classes where I could do artwork, learn things and hear about things. I got to spend my days learning new things and I didn't feel like an old man then. It made me forget the stereotypes and be me. I became useful and I taught people too. I felt like I had a surrogate family there too. We had parties and we also had jollies out by minibus.

There were also families who needed a bit of time away from caring from elderly relatives as well so I am sure they were glad that their relative had a lovely day away. It was wonderful for us all."

Widget looked angry. "What happened? It sounds like the ideal place."

Tailor shook his head. "Cuts. The Council cut the funding and got rid of our Centre. There are other places like mine that have closed as well. There was one in Aberystwyth which closed as well and they are now building a Tesco store where it used to be. They offered somewhere else but it was too far away. We were used to the old place, we didn't want change. For me the new one, I wasn't well enough to get on a bus and go there.

After the places were gone we all had nowhere to go and I suppose it was the same in Wales. I went from regularly seeing my friends to seeing nobody at all. Just because they didn't want to spend the money."

Widget frowned even more heavily. "That really

annoys me as I saw something on television that said that lots of money has been given to rich people. Why do they need it? Why didn't they step in and donate to build a smart new place for you? Everyone who is human will be old one day if they live that long. Disability can happen to anyone. Well, not for you, you are different now. You have us and as long as we can find an income we will have a lifetime home with us and we can do exciting things. If the Goblians don't kill us.

We went to Cardiff last month. That was exciting. I was attacked by a Goblian, that wasn't exciting. I won and he died and I lived so that was exciting in a way I suppose."

The Toymaker was still looking at the screen and a picture of the door reminded him. "Why don't we try to work out how to find this key that you are talking about. Do you have any keys or something about keys?"

Widget looked confused. "I think we should see if the Weaver of Dreams has left us any clues. She did mention that it was something to do with a key that belonged to Angel's parents. It has to be a big key and I think I have seen one somewhere."

Widget went to the table and climbed on the chair and reached onto the table where there she had seen a notebook. "If Angel has written something there may be a clue in the words. She gets influenced by the Weaver sometimes." She opened the book and went to the last page. "Yes, here we go. There is something here that might help."

As shadows fall as oft they will

And dreams are filled with madness

The gate must open or all is lost

Then man and Frixian will feel sadness

It will not open sans key Tolyne

Forged long ago, last century

By hand of man for justice's place

To unlock the way to gladness

Past future linked is what you need

And then the gate will open

Widget picked up the book and brought it back to the others. They went to the area under the stairs, cleared their table and set it out open so they could all look at it.

Tailor looked at the writing. "Why is there a bit of an odd word in the middle. Sans key Tolyne? Avec

key Tolyne? With key Tolyne. My key Tolyne?
Mon key Tolyne?"

Widget squealed and pointed at the stuffed toy
monkey which sat in a chair beside the table where
she had got the book. "Monkey!" Tailor looked at
the monkey. "By heaven! I made that monkey. The
Weaver showed me an image of me making that
monkey all those years ago.

How did it get here?"

Gadget poured them all a cup of tea. "That was
Angel's mother's monkey. She had had a monkey in
World War II when she was a little girl. The house
had got bombed and the people who helped to clear
up had stolen her toys, including the stuffed monkey.
So Angel found her one and gave it to her for her
seventieth birthday. When we cleared away her
mother's things after she died Angel kept the
monkey."

Tailor smiled. "Well I don't know how these things
work but I know that monkey and as I am the
Toymaker perhaps that is the Key Keeper? Now all
we need to do is find a key, a very old key that was
made last century and is something to do with
justice."

Widget piped up. "Easy peasy. There is an old key
in the TAVERN. It was Angel's father's. It was the

key that opened Leyton Police Station, justice. He had it as they pulled the old station down and built another one so they didn't have the door anymore. They didn't want it back. That is an old key."

Gadget picked up the book. "Tolyne scrambled is Leyton. For justice's place. We have the key. But surely it is just a key. What can link to the moon rock?"

Widget coughed. "Ah, well I forgot to tell you. I was told that a date was important. I took the Tardis to the moon, picked up some moon rock as the men were leaving and took it to where the key was going to be made. So it is made of moon rock. So technically it was forged in a volcano."

Gadget smiled. "Well I know of a story where something forged in a volcano wasn't good. Anyway, we have the key, we have the toy. If there is a gatekeeper or keykeeper then pehaps that needs a body. The monkey links past, present and I would guess future. So if we take the toy, and the key and get both of them to the gateway and do something then we may have an answer."

The three of them stepped out into the dark night. A small torch was all they had to see their way. Widget had the torch, Gadget clung to her and Tailor hung onto Gadget as he was still a little wobbly on his feet. Their magic kept them from getting muddy as they walked along the front of the house, crossed the wooden bridge and stepped into the garden.

The gentle rumble of the troll sleeping under the bridge and the babbling of the brook and the splashing sound of the water filled the evening silence.

The garden was dark. Widget had to find her way in the bubble of light shed by the small torch. But, she knew that garden very well and it didn't take her long to find the healing circle. The other two stepped beside her and looked down at the illuminated crystals set out in a circle at the base of a tree.

Tailor took the key and laid it in the middle of the pile of crystals. It glowed immediately and they all jumped back as the crystals began to glow as well and it hummed slightly. They glowed brighter and brighter until they could no longer look at them, the brightness hurt their eyes. Then the crystals dulled almost immediately, leaving the key glowing and illuminating the whole area.

Tailor reached out to pick it up but Widget caught his hand. "Be careful, that is glowing, that could be hot. Hot is bad. Remember you are a puppet now. You will burn."

Tailor grabbed a stick that was just poking into their circle of light. He held it out in front of him and pushed the key with it. It sparked into flame and he dropped it onto the crystals where it burst into flame and he dropped it onto the crystals where it burnt out, turned to ask and the ash blew away. "Yes, that is hot. I think we had better wait a little while." They sat on the bank and watched the key as it gradually lost its glow. Finally it was back to its rusty metal colour so Tailor tried again. He touched it with a stick again and nothing happened. He picked it up with the stick and nothing happened. So he reached out and took it off of the stick. It was warm but no longer hot. "Well, it looks like something has happened. What do we do now?"

A loud crack behind them made them all jump. The garden was illuminated by a bright orange light. They grabbed onto each other and they all screamed in unison. They looked at each other in the dim orange glow and turned around very slowly. Very very slowly as they really didn't want to see what was behind them.

What was behind them was them. And what was in front of the visitors was them. They were looking at themselves looking at themselves.

Tailor the second, who looked like the puppet they had just bid on on Ebay, held his hand up. "Don't panic. We are you in the future. We have our monkey here and the key, the key from the future.

You have the key from the past and the monkey from the past."

Widget the second smiled. "It has worked so far and it will work and we will very soon remember this as we have only read this in a book. We have taken the working travelling device as it is now fixed and gone into the future after the gateway is open. We have gone through the gateway and asked what we did to open it and the answer was that we had to bring a monkey from the past and a key from the past. We had to have a monkey from your future and a key from your future. If we bring them together on top of the gateway the Paradox Wave will trigger the lock and the gateway will open. The first spirit to be released is the one guarding the gateway. The one that keeps it shut, the Key Keeper. That spirit must be put into the monkey or it will kill anyone or anything it meets and would then put itself back into the gateway, shut it and keep it shut. We don't have much time as we shouldn't be here on your own timeline for too long. Let's do it."

Gadget took the monkey off of Widget the second and she and Widget walked together to the gateway. It was partially buried again under the leaf mold but it was still there. They stood either side of it and put both monkeys and both keys down together on top of the drain cover.

A white light and a burst of energy knocked them all off of their feet. There were sparks and a loud explosion rang out, waking everyone in the valley as it echoed across the swamp and through the woodland. Windows rattled as if they would break and then there was silence.

It was an eerie and foreboding silence as Tailor stepped forwards, not quite sure what he had to do. "Well this is the first time I've done this. I just hope I can."

Out of the gateway came a bright white light. It rose up to nearly eight feet tall and then it waivered in the still night air. It reached out towards the six puppets who were standing together, shaking. It reached out towards Tailor in particular who held out his hand and closed his eyes as the entity got closer. He was shaking in his shoes as the white light touched his fingers.

As he felt the energy touch him he realised it was a comfortable warm, like a lovely deep bath. It was not going to kill him so he opened his eyes again. He felt the power of the Gatekeeper and knew that it was a huge protective power.

He looked from face to face around the gathered group. He looked at the two monkeys. "Which monkey do I put it in?" Widget took a step forwards.

Tailor felt the energy reach towards her. "Stay where you are of it will take you. Don't move. I can't hold it forever and whatever it touches it is going to inhabit. Let me have an answer, past or future?"

Gadget looked around in horror as they hadn't talked about that. "I would say past. If you put it in the past one then it should then be in the future one."

Widget smiled. "I like the logic and I agree, the past one. Go on Tailor, let it go into the past one."

Tailor looked at Tailor two. "What do I have to do? Is there anything special. How do we put Frixians into puppets? You must know."

Tailor two laughed nervously. "You haven't done it yet and when you do I will know. Put the entity where it can touch the monkey and it can then be bound to it. I am sure that you will know."

Tailor reached out to Monkey one and the spirit disappeared into it like water into a sponge. It was gone and all was quiet.

The monkey got up and smiled at them. "Thank you and hello. You were very brave. I am free but I must forever guard the gateway. The gateway has some power from the crystals from the healing circle but it will not last forever. We can do all we can now but you must take the gateway to an ancient place of ancient power. Once then we can set up something to last."

In the darkness of London bombs were falling. The whistling sound and loud explosions filled everyone's life. Falling masonry, breaking glass and dust filled the air, choking and billowing into what was left of every house that had been blown to bits. Wood splintered and masonry fell. Treasured possessions and photographic memories fell in the mud and rubble to be tomorrow's rubbish. Fire raged along its path, indiscriminately destroying and it got closer and closer. He was only fur but he was loved. He knew he was loved. He had been with his little miss for a few years, looking after her, caring for her. But how did he know that? He had never known that. He hadn't known anything before. Not until now. Now he could feel and he was feeling what the monkey had felt and it was horrible. He was dusty and he was wet. Water thrown to put the flames out had made everything slippery and the flames had evaporated the water where it hadn't extinguished them. He looked down and thought how could she love him now. The fire got closer and he could feel its heat.

How could he feel? He had never felt before. He never thought before and all he could think was where was his little miss? Where had she gone?

Why wasn't he with her?

He heard voices, men were coming. Men were climbing over the rubble that had once been homes. Men were pulling out the living and the dead. But, one man wasn't helping. He was helping himself. He was taking the treasured possessions of those who had been bombed out and he was putting them in his pocket. He got closer and closer. He got to Miss' house and he came upstairs. There was no wall so monkey could see the room next door. The man reached for little miss' mother's treasured memories and put them in his pocket. He then reached out for monkey and monkey didn't like it.

Monkey screamed.

The man screamed, lost his balance and fell out of the hole in the wall and disappeared down into the flames of the house burning next door. He screamed then all was silence for him while the cacophony of the blitz continued.

Monkey was gone, he disappeared. He was no longer Miss's monkey, he was something else. He was swept up by a bolt of energy which took him from that house and that rubble.

He had shut his eyes and when he opened them he was in the arms of someone quite different. She was tall and white, glowing white. He looked down and saw her long white dress, long white hair and as she stroked his fur he felt happy. "Don't worry little one, you are safe. You will have a new life soon, you will be the Key master very soon. Let me show you something."

Monkey was spinning through something bright and then he wasn't. He was still with the woman who was keeping him safe but he could see his little miss. She was looking for him in the rubble and she was sad. She was crying. She wanted her monkey. He was sad too, he wanted to be with his miss.

"Little one" the woman spoke to him in a gentle voice. "in this timeline you were stolen by the man who just died. He died soon after anyway so the timeline was not disrupted too much. Now I am going to make you new again and I am going to put you in a shop. You are going to be bought by a young woman who is going to give you to your Little Miss for her seventieth birthday. Your little miss will not know it is really you but she will love you just as much. You have to leave now though. Only the toy can come through time, the Frixian that is you will have to take a step out of this world. I am showing you this so that you know and so that you know why you must go. This monkey must become the gatekeeper and there will be no room for two spirits in that body."

Monkey looked and monkey saw an old lady sitting with a wrapped package on her lap. Her face was still as kind and to him still as beautiful as it had always been. Her old hands pulled at the paper and as she ripped it away she saw her monkey. She hugged her monkey, remembering when she had lost him. She had a monkey again. A monkey to keep her company when everyone else had gone. A monkey to sit on her chair and be with her on dark nights when she was alone.

The white haired spiritual woman put him down. "You were that monkey again and you were with her all those years when she was growing up. You can be with her now until the time that the Gatekeeper needs the body. Then you must leave the body. I am not unkind. You will have to wait but there will be a body for you and you can be the first Frixian that the Toymaker puts into a body after the Gatekeeper. You shall have the body that the Toymaker has now when he moves into his new one. So be patient little one, all will be well.

It was the power of the wrong that was done to her by taking her monkey that gave us the power to be able to bring you to being the right vessel for the Gatekeeper."

Monkey Gatekeeper opened his eyes and he was in a garden. His body was a little different but the same.

He had spoken some words but now he could look around.

One by one Gadget two, Widget two, the monkey and Tailor two and their monkey and key faded away into the future leaving Gadget, Widget and Tailor standing in the garden with monkey standing beside them. There was silence as they took in what had just happened. Then a very spooky creaking of a large wooden door opening.

Tailor looked at the drain cover. It looked different to him now. It was as if there was a ghostly door standing over it. "Can you see that? Can you see that wooden door?"

Widget and Gadget shook their heads. They couldn't see anything other than the four of them standing in the torch light. Widget looked at Tailor who was staring intently at something they clearly could not see.

The monkey turned his head and looked from one to the other. "Only we can see it Toymaker. You have to see it so that you can bring Frixians through it when I open the door for you."

They walked back to the house in silence after the Keymaster had closed the door and locked it. They went back to the living room and back to their seats around the table. Monkey had now joined them.

Widget smiled. "Now we have a monkey friend as well. The number grows."

Monkey smiled. "Do I get a name?"

Widget thought about it. "You must have a name. What do you call yourself?"

Monkey smiled. "I don't. How about Keymon? Would that do?"

Widget smiled too. "Yes, that would do very well. So our numbers grow."

5 TALES OF THE TOYMAKER: THE PRINCESS AND THE PEACH

Abigail was a little girl who always thought that she was a princess. Her mother always treated her like a princess. Her father mostly treated her as a princess but sometimes he annoyed her by telling her that she wasn't. She acted like a princess and had all that she wanted and that was good enough for her.

She wore beautiful dresses which her mother sewed for her, sometimes staying up late at night to finish one off. She had a pretty sparkly tiara that she insisted on wearing every day. When she played in the garden she wore them. When she walked down the street she wore them. Those around her would know she was a princess, or so she thought and believed. The story starts at Christmas and like every other year of her life Abigail's Grandmother was coming to stay.

Her Granny was an old lady as Grannies often are. Abigail thought that she must be at least a hundred and as she was her Granny she had to be the oldest one alive. She had told her friends at school about her Grandmother and how she was the oldest person alive. She had got very cross that her teacher had dared to say that her Grandmother could not be that old. Abigail knew better and her teacher, as always when she disagreed with her was wrong.

The day of her Grandmother's arrival, Christmas Day, had come. The long wait was over. The house was cleaned. She liked that as her mother would clean in front of her. She could then step downstairs step by step as her mother swept the stair in front of her for her. She would walk slowly down the hallway as it as cleaned in front of her and then she would point to any dust that she saw and say. "You have failed me, you must try harder."

Her mother would then smile and remove the offending dust or dirt.

That had gone on for over a week and now the house was spick and span. The lights were clean, the skirting boards were clean and the carpet would be threadbare if they were cleaned any more.

Now tthey were all waiting for her in their best

clothes. The table was laid for tea. The best china was set out and the cruet set had been polished. Salt was in the salt pot. Pepper was in the pepper pot and sauces had been decanted into pretty glass pots on the table.

The tablecloth was washed, ironed and checked for any marks. It was as perfect as it could be. The cutlery had been washed and polished and laid out just so. One set for each course plus one for the bread.

Abigail had watched in wonder as he mother had folded the napkins into little flowers and tucked each one into a wine glass. One glass for red wine, one for water. It was all laid out beautifully.

Abigail had helped with the cooking too. She had cleaned out the mixing bowl. She loved to run her fingers over the inside of the bowl and then lick the mixture off of her fingers one by one. It tasted good. Sweet and sticky. It was her treat for helping. Today she had a double treat as there were scones to bake and a big cake. Not the Christmas cake and pudding. Those had been made ages ago. These were tomorrow cakes that would be eaten for tea.

The morning had been magnificent. She had sat next to the Christmas Tree and watched the television while her mother cleaned the room. Everywhere was decorated with sparkling tinsel and the tree had a beautiful fairy on the top of it.

Abigail was a little cross though. As Granny was visiting she had to wait to open the presents that Santa had left for her. This wasn't altogether fair and she knew it. She had been loud enough about it and as soon as her mother went out of the room she walked to the door and closed it. Then she went back to the pile of presents and picked out the first one with her name on it. She ripped the paper off of it and inside she found a cardboard box. The picture on the box showed a plastic horse for her doll. It was a brown one with a brown mane and tail. It had a matching nosebag, saddle and bridle and a broom. She just knew that her doll would enjoy cleaning the stable with that. Her dad had made her a wonderful stable and the horse she had already was tucked up warm in there.

Just at that moment her mother came back in. "Abigail, now what did I say?"

Abigail looked down at the horse. "I'm sorry mummy, I couldn't wait. Santa brought them last night. It is hard to wait until laster. It is Christmas Morning after all." She did feel a little guilty. It was a horrible cold feeling that she had done something wrong. It was her present though and it was unfair that she was made to wait when she could have opened her presents with her parents. She thought being nasty about the present just to make it her mother's fault and so that her naughtiness would be forgotten but just then Granny arrived.

She put the horse down and her mother quickly pulled out another piece of paper from the cupboard and wrapped it up again so that nobody would know. She wrapped it in the same as the other packages, put the tag back on it and put it back under the tree. "There, now nobody will know but don't you ever do that again."

Her mummy smiled at her and Abigail smiled back. She had got away with it but then again, it was Christmas.

She went to the door with her mother and there was Granny on the doorstep, wrapped in her big thick black coat with a fur collar. Her little pill box hat sat precisely on her neat black curls and her face was powdered with neatly applied lipstick finishing off her ensemble. There was no sign of any mascara or other make up. There might have been a little blusher or was that rouge? She couldn't be sure and she didn't want to look too closely. Granny's big black handbag was hanging over her arm and in her other hand she had a carrier bag full of wrapped presents.

Granny smiled, her eyes sparkling. "It is good to see you all. I have missed you."

Abigail's mother put her arms around her mother. "I'm sorry mum, it has just been so long."

Abigail laughed at her mother and gave her granny a hug. "I miss you too."

Granny smiled. "Well it seems that Santa has dropped some presents off at my house for you too. Would you like me to put them under the tree with your others?"

Abigail scowled as she knew once those presents were under the tree they would go off, have tea, she would settle in, they would chat and it would be hours before she could get to her presents. "No, I would like to open them and see what is inside."

Granny laughed. "Well in one of them you may find the gift of patience. It is up to your mother little one when we open our presents. Santa has brought me some as well and I' like to open mine too but not quite yet. What shall we do Janet? Shall we open them?"

Janet, Abigail's mother laughed and when Abigail wasn't looking she winked at her mother. "I'd love to open the presents but Jack ought to be here too. Shall I see if I can find him?

Granny smiled. "I think you had better. We wouldn't want him to miss out. Could you ask Jack to fetch my suitcase from the car first please? I didn't bring too much but I know he will say that I have. Where is he?"

Janet looked behind her as if she was going to see him miraculously appear. "You know I haven't seen him for an hour or so. I would imagine he is in his shed tinkering with his latest invention. I told him to keep the place tidy and not to touch anything so he ran away earlier. I think he thought that was the only way he'd keep the place tidy."

Granny laughed. "He is probably right, he is rather good at making a mess."

At that moment there was a loud "bang" from outside and as they ran into the garden they could see smoke coming out of the shed. It billowed up into the frosty air and out in a cloud from the front of the shed.

Janet screamed and ran for the shed, fearful for her husband. Granny tried to catch her but she was too quick. She ran across the snowy garden and got to the shed door as Jack staggered out. His hair was standing on end and he was covered in something that looked like soot. He was smiling which made his teeth really stand out starkly against the black of his face.

In his hand he grasped a large peach. It was mostly black from the soot on his hands but it was very clearly a peach and Janet could not remember buying any. He held it up and smiled. "I've done it. I've made a peach."

Granny glared at the be-sooted man in dismay. "My goodness, what on earth have you done?"

Jack smiled and waved the peach. "What I have done, what I have done is make a peach. Not grow a peach, I have made a peach."

Granny looked disappointed. "My dear, I hate to pour water on your celebrations but we have had peaches for years. I don't think that making a peach is anything new."

Janet turned to her mother. "Mother dear, Jack means that he made that peach. He manufactured it."

Granny's mouth slammed shut with a slightly audible clack from her false teeth. "Oh, I see what you mean now. Now that is very smart and something very special. I am sure that it will be able to feed lots of starving people."

Jack grinned from ear to ear. "Yes, now you know why it is so important. Of course there will have to be tests and I don't actually know if the peach is stable yet."

Abigail had been looking at the peach. "Can I have the peach?"

Jack smiled. "I am sorry dear. You cannot have this peach. I will buy you a peach when the shops are open again."

Abigail stamped her feet. She was already angry that she hadn't been allowed to open her presents and she was beginning to feel that she wasn't getting her own way at all. Her stamping didn't make any noise on the carpet and that annoyed her even more. "I want that peach. It is Christmas daddy, how can you say no!"

Jack smiled then tried to swallow the smile as he knew his daughter was totally serious but she did look very silly. "No my dear, I can say no very easily. You cannot have this peach. It is a special peach and it may harm you. Haven't I told you before that my experiments can be dangerous."

Abigail ran off to her room, tears falling from her eyes as she was angry that she had been denied the peach. She wanted that peach and her daddy was being very selfish.

Jack went back to his shed as he knew in his sooty state he would not be welcome in the house. He put the peach down on the table and dusted himself off. Janet went back into the house and thought about chasing Abigail upstairs but she had done that far too often. She knew it would only mean an hour or so of standing outside Abigail's room trying to get her out and giving Abigail an audience wasn't always the best solution to the problem. She had long learnt that leaving Abigail to come out on her own was far quicker as boredom was a more powerful weapon than anything she could say.

Granny went and sat in the living room in her usual chair near the Christmas Tree. She knew which chair was Jack's and she was certain to avoid that. She knew that Janet wouldn't mind her sitting on her chair as she would move to the sofa with Abigail for their Christmas viewing of the television. The television was on so she resigned herself to watching whatever was on as she didn't feel it was right to alter the channel. She wanted to talk to her family anyway. She looked the tree over and it met with her approval. She somehow loved to see some of the old decorations she remembered from years past. There was something reassuring about them. She looked around the room and then sat back hopeful of a sherry though not willing to ask for one.

Janet came in almost on cue with her sherry on a little tray. She had one for herself as well and sat down with her mother as she knew that everything was prepared and she had some time on her hands.

Granny smiled. "So you aren't upstairs trying to talk our little princess down?"

Janet shook her head. "No, it is Christmas. She will

be down soon enough as we have the presents."

Granny gave her a knowing look. "You are a good girl, you've learnt. I remember when you used to pander to that child's every whim. It will make her a better person."

They didn't hear their little princess as she stepped oh so quietly down the stairs. She moved step by step as she knew where every squeaky board was and she knew how to avoid them. She didn't want to be discovered as she had something on her mind. She had often crept downstairs when everyone was asleep. This was mostly because she didn't like being told when to go to bed so she would creep downstairs. Then she would get scared sitting downstairs on her own and she would creep quickly back. Sometimes she would creep half way down the stairs when her parents were watching television, sit on the stairs and watch the television through the crack in the door. Then she saw a film which scared her so she didn't do that for a very long time.

Now she put her knowledge to good use as she came down step by step. She could see her mother and Granny in the living room. She could see her father in the dining room trying to get the fire lit in the grate. She could see her chance and she went for it.

She got to the bottom of the stairs and tip toed down the corridor. She crossed the kitchen, carefully stepping on the mat. She knew if she did that it would muffle the sound of her steps. She put her hand on the back door latch and carefully lifted it. She opened it and went out into the snow covered garden.

She shivered as the cold air hit her and she wished she had thought about putting on a coat. She couldn't go back now so she would have to make do with being cold and trying not to think about it.

Step by step she made her way across the garden. She kept her steps in the same steps that her mother had made so that it was not obvious that she had gone that way.

The door of the shed was mostly off of its hinges and her father had propped it up with a piece of wood to stop it from swinging open. It was easy to move the piece of wood and as she did the door opened invitingly.

Inside the shed was full of very expensive looking equipment. She looked around in amazement as she had never been allowed inside. She didn't know what any of the equipment did but she knew it had probably been shiny before the explosion. There were a lot of buttons, they were all black now and she just knew that her father would tell her not to press them.

On the table was her prize, the peach. She didn't want to touch anything else, just that. She really wanted that peach.

She reached out her hand and picked it up. The soot from it came off on her hand. It felt a little tingly which was odd. She ignored it. She wanted it so she took it but that wasn't enough. She took a bite.

The peach was soft and juicy. The juice ran down her chin and she wiped it away with her sleeve, licking her lips with her tongue. She had never tasted anything quite like it. It was soft and sweet, perfectly ripe and delicious. So she took another bite, and another and another until only the stone remained. It was just a peach, well that was what she told herself as she was beginning to have some doubts and the certainly knew she would be in trouble. It didn't seem such a good idea anymore.

She smiled and put the stone back on the table. She was beginning to have doubts but she took a deep breath and convinced herself that she was right. "Well that will teach them."

She was just leaving the shed when she heard something which made her jump. She could hear scuttling, something was behind her. She turned around but she couldn't see anything. The room seemed still and empty. The stone was on the table and everything was as it had been.

Then with a crack the stone cracked. A green shoot grew from it and immediately she thought of Jack and the Beanstalk and wondered if it was going to start growing upwards.

She shut her eyes and opened them again. It was still growing and it was growing faster now. The little shoot now had leaves. Then she noticed that the scuttling sound had come from the other side of the stone. A root had already started growing. Both carried on growing and had begun to fill the shed. Abigail backed away and ran out into the garden.

She ran to the house and through the kitchen door, slamming it shut behind her. As she was just about to walk away and pretend it wasn't her, her father came out of the dining room. "Abigail, whatever is the matter?"

Abigail's mouth slammed shut as she realized what she had done and what she had caused. More importantly than that she would have to explain to her father why she had eaten his peach. At that point she decided that perhaps eating it wasn't the best thing to do and certainly not a good idea.

She didn't have to though as his questions were answered by a green tendril which poked through the keyhole.

Abigail ran to her father and took his hand. "I have

been a very naughty girl and I am very sorry."

The tendril grew and grew into the room and Jack grabbed her to pull her away from an exploratory tendril which had branched off and was reaching for her. "Go away!" He shouted as he snatched his daughter away just in time.

The door flew from its hinges, smashed by the weight of the plant behind it. The foliage then tumbled into the room and writhed on the floor. It squirmed about and the table stand which displayed an antique jug that Janet loved so much tumbled to the floor. The jug was launched off of it and smashed on the floor. Water spilled onto the floor and the bouquet of flowers that Jack had bought for Janet were strewn across the carpet.

There wasn't time to be upset about it as the tendril was unstobbable. It grabbed Abigail firmly around her waist and lifted her up out of her father's reach. It then retreated at full speed, carrying her through the door, across the lawn with her father in hot pursuit before she flew backwards through the door of the shed. She couldn't scream as she was too frightened. She reached her arms out trying to grab her father's arms but the plant was too quick.

She didn't see what was in the shed but her father did. The peach stone was on the table but it had grown too and the crack in it was large enough for the plant and Abigail to disappear into it and the crack shut with a loud snap. The stone then shrunk to normal size and regrew its peach around itself.

It was dark, Abigail was alone and there was no vine around her. She had felt it let her go. She was standing in the darkness and had no idea where she was. The air smelt cold. The floor was covered with a carpet. She didn't smell as though she was outside. She felt around herself in the darkness, holding her arms out with her hands open. She felt in front, at the back and to the sides. She then felt down in front of her and her fingers touched something solid. It was flat on top and she followed the edge and realised that it was square and had four legs, it was a table. She then felt on top of it, hoping to find a torch. The first thing she came across was a small box, then what felt like a candle and a candlestick. The box was a box of matches, she had seen one of them before. She carefully slid the box drawer open and felt inside and felt the little pieces of wood. Her hands were shaking and it wasn't easy. She carefully lifted one out. She had not been allowed to play with matches but she had seen her father light the candles on her birthday cake so she knew what he had done. She tipped the box to strike the match and all the matches fell out. She gasped in horror as she realised that had probably just lost her the chance of a second chance if the first match didn't light. She had no option, she took the match and dragged it swiftly along the striking strip. Nothing happened. She then felt the match, turned it around and tried again. The match crackled and she was rewarded with a golden light which illuminated a globe around itself. She put the candle in the stick and lit it. She then picked up all the matches that were on the table and put them carefully back in the box.

She could now see the table. It was bright green and its paint was oily and thick. One the table as well as the candlestick there were other things she had missed in the darkness.

There was a necklace which was old. Not antique and valuable old, just worn out old. It had a leather chord which had obviously been well worn. The pendant was a metal disc with a spiral on it. The spiral was distinct though worn. From outer to inner or inner to outer, she didn't know which and something in her child like mind she hoped that if she traced it she would be magically taken home. She tried but nothing happened. She didn't know if it was real brass or bronze but as it appeared useless she slipped it over her neck and looked at the other things. There was a crystal point like she had seen in a shop her mother had taken her to once. Her mother had said it was for those people who tell fortunes or do spiritual things. She wasn't altogether sure what that meant but they had been a pretty collection in the box on the table. The was a metal ring which she slipped on her finger and a tiny metal bottle. She almost missed the acorn with a crystal stuck into it which had a loop to make it a necklace, if it had a chain. She looked at each of them and rolled them between her fingers while thinking. There was also a small leather drawstring bag. They didn't seem to be laid out in any order and she had no idea what they did if indeed they did anything They were just placed on the table.

She picked up the candle and walked to her right and then to her left.

Whatever direction she went here was still darkness and the room seemed to go on forever. She then went back to the table. "Oh dear" She said to herself. "What shall I do?"

She picked up the other things and put them in the little bag and put it in her pocket. "Well if they are here they must be here for a reason. I've seen the films and I've read the books. Each one will have a purpose and all I have to do is work out what and I can go home."

"Of course they are." The voice came from her right and out of the candle's glow. "They are here for the purpose of being where their owner put them."

She visibly jumped and turned to her right so that the

candle light extended in that direction. She moved the candle as she didn't see anyone there. Then she thought perhaps she didn't actually want to see what was there.

What she saw standing there was a small black goat with white spots and tiny horns. He looked at her with his big brown slit eyes and tilted his head to the side slightly to get a better view of her.

She was fascinated but afraid as well. "You can't talk, you are a goat." She stated indignantly and glared at him.

The goat stamped his foot but took a step back out of reach of the little girl as he was suddenly scared of her. "You can't tell me if I can talk or not. I speak, that is that. Now say sorry for being so rude or I will tell my father and he will butt you so hard you will learn to fly. I've never met a talking doll before either. So we are both experiencing something new. If indeed where you come from goats do not talk."

Abigail looked stunned. "I am sorry, where I come from goats do not talk. They bleat and are kept in farms. I have had a bad day and I am very scared so I hope that you won't bring your father to butt me. I think that might hurt."

The goat licked his leg, straightening a bit of fur. "Well where I come from, here, they do and as you are now where I come from that is that and

that is all you need to know."

Abigail smiled at the little goat. "Are you here to help me?"

The little goat snorted. "I am here and curious because you are here. Why should I be here for you? You are a selfish, rude and dishonest little girl who is a thief and a liar."

Abigail's mouth snapped shut. "Nobody speaks to me like that. I am not."

The goat made a noise somewhat like a raspberry. "You are. You are totally rude and totally nasty. You think that everyone is here for your amusement and you have no thought for others. Why should I help someone like you? Why do you assume that I am here to help you?"

Abigail looked stunned. "You can't speak to me like that. You are very rude and I am a princess."

The goat looked at her sideways. He saw the princess' fine dress. He saw the princess' tiara. "Well you are not a princess of here and I feel sorry for any subjects who might have you as a Queen one day."

Abigail stamped her foot. "I am a princess wherever

I happen to be. I demand that you take me home!"

The goat turned away from her. "You aren't coming to my home, you are nasty."

Abigail frowned. "I didn't say I wanted to go to your home. I want to go to my home. I want you to take me."

The goat stood silently for a little while. "I cannot do that and I have a lot to do today."

Abigail began to cry. The tears fell down her face and dripped onto her dress. The satin was easily marked by the tears and at any other time she would have been very, very upset. Today she didn't notice. Her hands were over her face and she was crying and crying."

The goat just watched her. "You can cry all you like. I am a goat. I was a goat and I will always be a goat. So I can't help you. Don't be stupid, I don't even have hands. I have goat things to do. You have been amusing but you are getting boring now."

Abigail looked at the goat in horror. "Then why are you here?"

The goat looked bemused. "I'm here because I live here. I walk this way often and I look at the things on the table and wonder what they are for. Now you have taken them. I don't know if you should or if you did it because you could. That could be bad or good for you. For me it doesn't matter, I

just live here but they are things seen by many people so that they are gone, that is not good for me. Don't go and explode because of it. I would feel guilty then for not stopping you. The Witch may well come and turn you into something for taking them if she likes them too."

Abigail looked horrified. "I'm a child, you can't talk to me like that. I have been grabbed by a plant, dragged to a strange land and now I need to find my way home. Dinner will be served soon and I don't want to miss it. In all of the stories the heroine comes to a strange land. What she finds she needs. She then saves the world as a byproduct of getting home." She took a breath.

The goat looked at her in earnest. "You said you were a princess. Princesses have responsibilities as they have to grow up to be Queens or are married off to help someone else rule. They don't have time for fun and they certainly do not lie and steal. You are nothing but a common thief and a beggar or you should be. You can put fine clothes on but you are still a nasty girl. You have come to where I live and taken things that do not belong to you."

Abigail's eyes got wider and wider. "How dare you talk to me like that!"

The goat shook his head. "I can talk to you any way I choose and there isn't anything you can do about it." Abigail stamped her foot again.

The goat seemed to grin. "You would make a good goat. Perhaps the Witch will turn you into one. You would learn manners if you had to wait for hay."

Abigail got even more angry. "Why would I want to be a goat?"

The goat wagged its tail. "You had better stop there. You have already proven yourself to be rude. Don't add insulting me to that. Just because I can't take you home doesn't mean that I'm a bad goat. You have turned up here, stolen, insulted a local and you now expect me to do something I cannot do just because you want me to? Grow up child. Or at least be a child. Children are supposed to be good at this sort of thing. You are just nasty about it and I wouldn't be if I were you. You are trapped somewhere far from your home with nowhere to go and no idea about how to get home. To find out how to get home, if there is a way, you are going to have to ask and investigate. Or is there no way home? I'm a goat, I can't tell you, before you ask or are rude to me again."

Abigail looked at the empty table. "Do you think I should put them back? I've read stories where someone finds things that they need and they are magical."

The goat bowed its head. "Do you think they are magical? Why do you think they are there?"

Abigail actually scratched her head. It fascinated her as she hadn't done anything like this before. She had seen people on films do it though, or thought she should have. Then she hadn't been trapped somewhere that she couldn't get home from without her parents either. Not that she had been trapped anywhere with her parents either. "Well I think they must be or they wouldn't be there. I think they were there so that I can find my way home. That is what happens isn't it? If you need something it will be there for you."

The little goat itched its back lag with its teeth. "You are assuming a lot.

Firstly that you are important enough for anyone to leave anything for you. Secondly that it isn't just things that were important to and individual that someone left to be spiritual and then forgot about so didn't come back."

Abigail suddenly felt very small and very alone. "In the stories I have read when someone goes to a place like this in the way I came here they find things that will get them home. They have a short, frightening but not actually dangerous adventure and then it is all over and they go home."

The goat was listening with interest. "Why do you say that it will be like that? Life is interesting. It is like looking for a blade of grass in a field that is tasty. There are many experiences you must experience to be who you are and to enjoy the good ones. Most importantly it teaches you to be you.

I might help you. I might not. If I don't help you then you'll work it out somehow or you'll have to learn to live here. If you are nasty then nobody is going to take you in so you will starve and freeze in the winter. It is nearly winter here so if I were you I'd be nice to people."

Abigail stood in silence and looked at the little goat. She put her hand in the pocket and felt the little bag of things she had taken. Her hand then involuntarily moved to the necklace she had taken. "I didn't think, I just picked them up as I thought they were relevant. What should I do with them?"

The small goat looked around. "Well they aren't yours but they have been there a very long time. Perhaps they were put there for you. There is no way of knowing. You found them but they weren't lost. That is the difference between finding something and stealing something. I suppose. Stealing is bad and someone will be very unhappy that the stolen item is gone. I like many other people look at those things quite often. We will miss them so although they do not belong to us they are in a way ours. There is no reason why those things will help you to get home. I am sure if you are prepared to put them back when you have finished then my friends and I wouldn't mind you borrowing them."

Abigail thought for a while. "Well, if your friends came along and helped me to get home they will make sure that I put the things back. Can I meet your friends?"

The small goat thought about it. "Yes, I will ask them. Come with me.

You don't seem to have anything else to do at the moment."

Abigail smiled and wiped her tears. "Thank you."

The little goat wagged its tail. "That's better."

They set off and the carpet seemed to go on forever. Step after step they walked and all the time Abigail was trying to think of what to do.

The small goat skipped along. Sometimes jumping sideways, sometimes skipping around and coming back to stand beside her.

He looked up at her, his dark eyes bright. "The first friend we are going to see is the grey bear. He may or may not help you."

The carpet had become green and less flat. There were mounds in the carpet and on one of these mounds a stick poked through the pile. As they walked further more sticks pushed up through the carpet and these sticks became trees as they grew. The carpet became grass. Abigail wasn't totally sure when the carpet had become grass but it had.

The small goat stopped. It then bleated very loudly. The goat waited and then there was a growl in the distance.

A small grey bear walked slowly into the clearing where they were standing. He stood up on his back legs and then sat down and looked at them. "Well, is this lunch?"

The small goat made a sniffing noise. "No, this is a person who is stuck here. She just appeared. She is irritating and I'd rather she didn't stay in our world or there will be trouble. Can you help me to get rid of her?"

Abigail glared at the goat who looked up at her. She saw him wink and then she understood so she stood very still and waited.

The grey bear wiggled his nose and sniffed the air. "I don't seem to have much else to do at the moment."

The goat wagged his tail. "She has taken the things from the table. Before you get cross, like I did, listen. She thinks that she needs them to get her home. So I'm going along with her to make sure that she doesn't steal our things and only uses them if she has to. Do you want to come along too?"

The bear growled. "You took the things? That was nasty of you. But, if you are prepared to only borrow them then that is a little more fair. I would go with you but I have to finish a job first. If you help me, I will help you."

Abigail was about to speak but the goat stamped on her foot. She looked down and was too busy rubbing her foot to answer.

The goat tilted his head. "So, what is this job you would like help with?"

The bear smiled. "My shelter is leaking and I keep getting wet. I would like to fix it before I go anywhere."

The goat looked at Abigail. "Would you help?"

Abigail stopped hopping and being dramatic and glared at the goat before she thought about it and nodded."

The shelter was between three trees. It was a ramshackle mix of bits of wood balanced together and most of it had fallen down. Abigail looked at it.

"You need string to fix this. Do you have string?"

The bear looked down at the ground. "I don't have that sort of thing. I am a bear."

Abigail stuck her lip out. "You have built a house so you are not the average bear."

The bear laughed. "Well that I am."

Abigail smiled. "I forget that I am not home. Where I live bears do not speak and goats do not speak either. I can help you to make your house stand up."

She took the necklace from around her neck. It was on a leather thong and as she untied it she realized she had quite a long piece of thong. She took it to the wood and then carefully took the planks and sticks down and found some that were the same length. They were the longest ones. She piled half of them up like a teepee and then tied them firmly at the top with the thong so that they made a firm structure. She left a long piece hanging. It seemed that the thong was somehow longer than it had been around her neck. She then took the boards and put them around the poles. She then picked up the other half of the long poles and dug them into the ground the pulled their tops up to where the other sticks were tied and tied the lot together. There was just enough thong. The result was a stronger structure big enough for the bear to go inside. It was just like the tent she and her friend Jenny had made with Jenny's brother in their garden. That had been a good day until she had fallen out with Jenny. Thinking about it, perhaps she had been a little silly and it had been nearly three years since she had spoken to her. Perhaps if she got back she would see if Jenny still wanted to be her friend.

The bear went straight in and sat down. He looked around and pushed the walls carefully with his paws before giving it a harder shove. The walls held firm, the wind kept out and the bear smiled. This will give me a lovely place to spend my winter sleep. Thank you. I will now help you." The little grey bear fell in with them and they walked on.

Abigail looked around. The trees wore their autumn colours, golds and browns. She hadn't noticed that happening but it had. The leaves crunched under her feet and the air smelt chilled and damp. The rich smell of the loam filled her nose and as the wind blew she wished she had a coat. The littlegoat was right, she was going to have a cold winter if she couldn't get home.

She reached into the bag and took out the things. The

bear and goat looked over her arm to see what was in there. "An interesting collection and I've absolutely no idea what to do with them."

The little goat looked up at her. "Well like with the string, you never know what anything is useful for. Or they may not be useful at all. They may just be the reason why we are coming with you. For now let us just enjoy the journey."

The woodland was a glorious array of oranges, browns and burnt ochre. It stretched as far as they could see but they couldn't see too far because of the bushes which held onto their fading leaves as well. Their glorious last blast of colour was their farewell to the year. The cleansing fire before skeletal barrenness of winter and the bursting buds of spring.

Abigail hadn't thought about it before. She had never noticed the trees changing colour or the way the wind moved them. She hadn't noticed the crunch as her feet stepped on the piles of drying leaves. She liked the sound.

The sounds and scents of the forest filled her senses. It confused her and excited her at the same time. She was miles from home but she didn't feel afraid.

The little goat trotted along beside her. The grey bear on her other side. They wandered through the woodland not really knowing where they were going but hoping that it was the right direction.

The woodland opened into a rolling pasture which led down to a bubbling and swirling river. The water danced and bounced over rocks in its way. It was wide, about ten feet at its narrowest. The river wasn't deep and it was clear as crystal. The current wasn't too strong so they were able to step into it.

The water felt sharply cold around their ankles. It soaked their legs but it was a pleasant feeling, not a frightening one. They had to be careful as the rocks were very slippery. They had to hold onto each other and Abigail laughed as she nearly lost her footing. It wouldn't be deadly to fall but it would certainly be wet and she did not want to be wet for the rest of the day.

They stepped up onto the bank for a while and just watched the stream, sitting together enjoying a moment. Abigail could have told them she wanted to go on but actually she didn't want to. She was very happy where she was. Finally she stood up. "Well I suppose we ought to head off."

The other two got up and they headed off along a track which had seen plenty of feet, hooves and paws over the years. It was dug down about a foot and the rolling countryside swooped away from it in all directions.

They walked on and on and the autumnal sun warmed them as they walked. The sun was behind them and their shadows were getting longer. They walked on and as they walked they saw a wooden cottage in the distance. They got closer and saw it had a sign outside. It was a little hotel for travelers called "The Traveller's Rest".

Abigail looked at the building nervously. "What do we do? We can't stay out all night. We'll have to get a room won't we?"

She went in first, the other two following closely behind. The door was old and slightly dusty. When she knocked there was a slight cloud of dust which floated into the air and hung there momentarily like a collection of magically infinitely small fairies. Then the door opened and Abigail stepped backwards.

There was a man at the door, a very big and very hairy man. He was a good six foot six and his head touched the door lintel. He had a huge bushy beard and huge bushy hair. His coat was a startling bright green and his boots a very bright orange. He smiled a huge beaming smile and opened the door further. "Good evening, do you want a room?"

Abigail was lost for words. She smiled and nodded.

The man looked down at her. "Well we are twenty

Ildas a night. That would have to be in advance."

Abigail looked down at her wrist and pulled off her bracelet. She had been given it by her mother and father and she really liked it. They couldn't sleep outside all night so she had to do something. She held it out to the man in the doorway. "Would this be enough of a payment?"

The man looked at the bracelet and took it off of her. "Yes, that will be fine. I'll show you all to your rooms."

Once they were sitting in Abigail's room after being shown to their own and then coming back to see her there was an uneasy silence. It was broken by the small goat. "Why did you give him your bracelet? You could have given him one of the things from the table."

Abigail rubbed her now empty wrist. "I gave him the bracelet because the things on the table are not mine to give. The bracelet is. It was a gift but I'd rather see them again than have the bracelet."

The little goat thought for a moment. "You have changed. That is good."

Abigail put her head on her pillow after her friends had gone to bed. The pillow was soft and plumped up. The mattress was equally soft and there was a huge feather quilt she could pull up over herself. It was very heavy and it took her a while to get used to it.

She lay in the coolness of the sheets and looked around the room. It was plain and there was a lot of wooden decoration in the room. The walls were paneled wood, the floor just boards. There was a single wardrobe which somehow seemed very intimidating and a perfect place to keep a monster. There was a table with a wooden bowl on it and a chair. Other than that there were no other furnishings.

The goat had been shown to a stall downstairs and the bear had been shown to a room which was plain with only a bed in it. This was truly an interesting world Abigail thought.

As she drifted off to sleep she wondered if the act of sleeping might take her home and if this was only a dream.

When she woke up in the morning, still on the bed, still in the room she knew that it wouldn't be as easy as that.

She got up and there was an enormous breakfast waiting for her on the table in the dining room. The large man stood next to it and brought her a pot of tea. He brought her toast and when she had finished he cleared it all away. His voice seemed deeper than the night before. "Would you like something else?"

Abigail smiled. "No thank you, I really enjoyed that and I can't eat another thing. Where are my friends?"

Was it her imagination or did the man look a little nervous when she asked the question. She was immediately suspicious. "They left in the night. They told me to tell you that they were going to continue on the journey and you can catch them up."

Abigail was really nervous now. She didn't need to think about it. She knew that there was no way that they would have been able to go on without her to continue the journey. She was the journey. She bit her tongue to calm her nerves. "Do you serve lunch?"

The man smiled. "Yes, today we do. We will have a roast dinner today.

With all the trimmings." He smiled.

Abigail tried really hard not to react and her head raced with horrible thoughts. She knew she wouldn't normally ask what type of meat so if she asked it would be obvious that she was suspicious. She was worried that if she did ask then he would say goat meat.

She got up and thanked the man and when she went

outside she could see the footprints where they had arrived but there were no footprints of the goat and bear leaving.

She went back to her room and listened very carefully. She couldn't hear anything so she started opening doors. She went to their rooms, they weren't there. She opened door after door and the place seemed impossibly big inside. Then she opened one that made her stop in her tracks. The room was full of cages and the cages were full of animals. Two of the animals she recognised as her friends. They were in big cages with big padlocks.

She looked around the room and there were only cages and animals. In the corner there was a huge axe and she really didn't like the look of that. On a hook there was a set of keys and she was definitely glad to see them. She looked at the floorboards, they were old and they would creak. So she walked very carefully, using all her skill. She stepped inside and went to the keys and carefully unlocked the padlocks asking everyone to wait. She let everyone out and when she gave the signal they all leapt from their cages. There were tigers, lions, kangaroos and all manner of animals who rushed out of the door and down the stairs.

There was a howl from the man downstairs but the animals didn't stop. They weren't afraid of him now.

There were too many of them and they knocked him over and as he ran past the wolf ripped his throat out.

Abigail and her friends ran as well. Down the stairs, through the front door and out onto the grass outside. They didn't stop, they kept going until the building was a long way behind them.

When they were far enough away that they felt safe they sat down to rest. The little goat folded his legs under his body and put his head on Abigail's lap. The grey bear sat down beside her and they sat together for a while until the goat spoke. His voice was shaky. "I never want another night like that. I didn't sleep a wink in that cage. Thank you for saving us. It was very brave of you."

The bear looked at her. "Well I didn't sleep either. It was horrible." Abigail looked down at the grass which was surprisingly not just grass. There were little flowers and little ferns amongst the grass blades. She ran her fingers through it. It was soft and springy. "I don't know what we should do next. There are no clues here. Nothing makes sense."

The little goat looked up. "Well what do you want to do?"

Abigail looked around at the countryside. "I don't know really. I was in a great hurry to get home but now I'm not so sure."

The little goat shook his head. "You have to find your way home. You have parents who will be worried about you."

Abigail frowned. "I have absolutely no idea how to get home."

The little goat thought for a while. "Well we will have to go and have some sort of adventure no doubt. I am sure we can find a way to get you home. There must be someone who knows a way."

Abigail looked at him. "Well I had thought to start with that whatever happened my just reverse itself or that my daddy would sort it out and I'd be whisked back there. That hasn't happened yet so I think you could be right.

Do you know of anyone?"

Just as she said that there was a dark shadow which swept across the landscape. It turned day to night as it filled the sky. They all looked up in horror and above them was a huge dragon. It blocked out the sun and its huge wings spread out as it flapped them slowly and soared through the air.

The companions dived for cover as best they could. They used what they had available and with a flap of its wings the dragon was gone. It wasn't interested in them at all.

It took a while for them to stop shaking. Abigail looked at her two companions. "That sort of exciting I can live without."

The little goat was still trembling as he thought about it again. "Exciting is not a word I would use. Do you still like it here?"

Abigail looked down at her shoes. "There are bad things in my world too. Horrible things. People are doing horrible things to each other. I don't like my world, it isn't a good world to grow up in. People don't play fair and there is war and murder and crime." She sat down with a bump. The little goat laid down beside her and put his soft furry head on her lap. She stroked it and he seemed as though he'd gone off to sleep. The bear came back to sit beside her as well.

He spoke in a soft growly voice. "If I was lost I would go and see someone who deals in magic. They might have a spell to find your way."

Abigail looked at him in surprise. "I hadn't really thought about that. Then I don't really know your world so I wouldn't know about things like that. Do you know where to go?"

The bear thought for a moment. "We could go and see the Witch. She might be able to help."

Abigail looked terrified. "What you mean actually go and see a witch? A hat wearing, long nosed, broomstick riding witch?"

The bear looked confused. "You have never met a witch have you? They may be different here but she is a beautiful woman who is kind to everyone and looks after nature. She also does spells and has a good business going doing people's housework for them. Of course she is also mad as a mad thing and batty as a batty thing. The other witches have nothing to do with her as she has a habit of turning anyone who annoys her into a toad. So there could be some perils on our adventure."

Abigail laughed. "I should say! I don't want to be turned into a toad."

The bear sighed. "Well the way to avoid that is simple. Don't annoy her." Abigail smiled. Perhaps I should leave the talking to you?"

The bear shook his head. "I don't much fancy being turned into a toad either. When Prancing Hooves there wakes up we could head that way and go and see if she can help."

Abigail looked down at the little goat. "Prancing Hooves, is that his name?"

The bear laughed. "No, but I don't know his name

so it seemed something to say."

Abigail looked at the bear quizzically. "Well I don't know your name either. What is your name?"

The bear smiled. "Some call me Archie. I like Archie so you can call me that too if you like."

Abigail smiled. "Pleased to meet you Archie."

Just then the goat woke up. "They call me Lemmie if you want to know my name. But Goat does just as well. Have you thought of something?"

Abigail smiled again. She was doing a lot of that. That was something she hadn't genuinely done often in her own world. "Well although I really like this place I must go home I suppose. So Archie here has come up with the idea of going to see the Witch. What do you think?"

Lemmie looked up at her. His dark eyes a little sad. "I'd try not to think too hard about that one. She is a mad old bat who would probably turn me into a toad without even waiting for me to be annoying. Or dinner. I don't want to be dinner."

The bear laughed. "You don't know anything about her do you?"

Lemmie bleated. "I don't have to. Witch says it all for me."

Abigail's feet were hurting. They had walked for miles through rolling countryside and tangled woodland. Sticks were tangled in her hair and her face was muddy. Her beautiful dress was torn and her tiara was missing. She had lost it long ago but she didn't bother to go back to look for it. She had just kept walking. She didn't really want to be a princess anymore anyway. Her friends kept walking too but each step took them closer and closer to the Witch.

It was nearly night when they came to a small cottage in a clearing in the forest. It was much like the other forests they had passed through and the cottage looked like any other cottage. It was small and neatly kept. The paintwork was immaculate. The satin green shutters were neatly clipped back. The windows were polished and plants grew immaculately in baskets.

There was a small fence around the immaculately tended garden. The gate was green, like the shutters and the gravel path was sparkly white.

She walked up to the door and stood in front of it. Images of wizened old ladies with hooked noses and warts ran through her mind. Of course along with the imagery of pointed hats and broomsticks. She had to smile as she looked around the door and saw a broomstick there. It was one of those classic besom types. That above all things made her feel nervous but she knew she had to knock on the door so she took a deep breath and tapped on the door very quietly in as polite a manner as she could manage.

Lemmie laughed. "You'll have to knock a little louder than that." She didn't need to as the door opened. At first a crack and then wider.

Silently it swung back to reveal a neat hallway. The floorboards were polished and the half moon table had a vase of daffodils on it.

The witch towered over her. She was tall, blonde and dressed in a pretty lacy dress with a neat apron which was tied around her neck and around her slim waist. The dress was white, the apron blue. It had pockets in the front but these were flat and neatly pressed.

The witch smiled. Her immaculate lipstick was lustrous red. As she looked down at them and blonde curls bounced around her face. "Hello guests, what brings you to my door today?"

Abigail couldn't help it but smile back but her smile soon fell from her face as the most hideous creature stepped from a room off of the hallway. He was part beast and part man. His face was covered by a thick bushy beard which partly concealed his heavy brow and large protruding nose. He was very tall, much taller than the witch. His hunched back pushed his face forwards and his long gangly arms were clutching a frying pan.

The witch turned towards him. "We have guests. Please will you put the kettle on."

The beast grunted. "Very well, I will." He shuffled off.

The witch turned back to her guests. "Now, please come in and follow me. I baked a cake today so you have chosen the right day."

Abigail tried to smile but the image of the beast seemed to leer over any welcome that the witch was offering. She turned to Lemmie and realised that the bear had disappeared.

Lemmie tilted his head. "He has just gone off for a while. He is scared of the Witch and that beast. Don't worry, he won't be far away." Lemmie cast a glance at the Witch who was watching intently.

Abigail stepped into the hallway. The house was warm and smelled of roses as she followed the Witch into what looked like a living room.

There was a small sofa and a winged back flowery chair. A dark wood coffee table had a single leather bound book on it. The curtains were chintz. The carpet was flowered. The place was immaculately clean and the fire was laid for lighting later. There was a mantelpiece above the fire and a line of white and blue ornaments looking down at her. They were smooth effigies of people doing tasks. Ther was a fisherman with a fish. A woman matched him with a basket of fish. An angel with a bowl in front of her and a boy with a goat.

The Witch indicated the sofa and Abigail sat down as politely as she knew how. Lemmie laid down on the floor beside her as the Witch left the room with a cheery "Ill go and fetch the tea for you."

In the kitchen the Witch walked through the door just as the beast was reaching for the dainty cups and saucers where were set neatly on a shelf on the dresser. She coughed and he stepped away. His chunky hands a fraction of a distance from the delicate china. "Now you know you aren't very good with the china."

The beast looked sad and looked down at his big hairy feet. "I try to help.

I break too much. I'm sorry."

The Witch smiled. "You don't have to be sorry. One day we'll break the curse and you'll be back to your old self. It would be interesting to meet your old self. But I love this self so don't worry about it. I read the cards this morning and I think that little girl in there might be able to help us. You'd like that wouldn't you?"

The beast grunted. "I don't like how I am but I do like my life here with you. Are you sure we need to break the curse? Shouldn't we be content to be how we are?"

The Witch smiled kindly. "The neighbours look down on you and your old friends don't visit. Your father and mother don't want to know you and people keep on turning up to kill you as they must slay the beast. Surely it is not a good way to live and it would make for a more peaceful life if you weren't the beast."

The beast looked down at himself. "And you don't like the way I look?" The Witch smiled. "I love you for who you are."

The beast smiled. "Good, well if this little girl can help then that will be the way things should be."

The Witch took down the cups and set them out on a flowery tray. The crockery was white with red flowers on it. She took the teapot and poured in some water, swished it around and tipped it into the sink. She then took the oriental tea caddy, took the top off, took an ornate silver spoon and measured out the tea leaves into the pot. "One for you, one for me, one for each of them and one for the pot. There you go." She poured in the water and put a floral tea cozy over the pot.

She went to the cupboard and pulled out a large chocolate cake and set it onto a plate. She then took a cake knife from the drawer and cut generous slices for everyone. "Now are you coming in to sit with us?"

The beast shook his head. "No, I will scare your guests and they won't be able to think clearly. I had better stay here. Can I have some cake? I love your cake and I love you."

The Witch smiled and passed a large piece of cake to him and put it on a slightly chipped plate. She then took a battered much from the draining board by the sink and put some milk into it. She then poured him a mug of tea and left him to enjoy his tea and cake.

He took the mug and plate and went to sit on his chair by the window in the kitchen. He could see the pretty bluebirds and butterflies of different colours flittering around in the garden.

The Witch carried the tray into the room and set it down on the coffee table. She put milk into cups for Abigail and herself and poured the tea. "Do you take sugar?"

Abigail nodded. "Yes please, I would like one spoonful please."

The Witch put a spoonful of sugar into the cup and put the spoon into the saucer and passed it to Abigail. She then passed a slice of cake to Abigail and set one on the side of the table for Lemmie. She poured tea into a bowl she had brought with her and set that beside the cake for him. She then sat on the sofa beside Abigail. "It is lovely to meet you."

Abigail finished her mouthful. She was very conscious of her manners and tried to remember all the things that she knew were right. She sat neatly. She picked up the spoon and stirred her tea and took a mouthful. It washed down the cake and gave her time to think about what she was going to say.

"It is lovely to meet you too. I hope that you do not mind us visiting."

The Witch smiled. "It is always a pleasure to receive guests. We get so few these days." She looked sad but cast a sideways glance momentarily to make sure that Abigail had seen this sadness. "Since my husband was cursed he has had a few problems with his friends and family visiting."

Abigail tried to put on her most sympathetic look. "That is awful. What happened? If you don't mind me asking."

The Witch crossed her delicate legs, her pretty white buckled shoes catching the sunlight. "It was a few years ago now. Marikus, who you now see as the beast is the son of King Lars. He was a dashing and brash youth then. He was so handsome that women would queue up in the hope that he would notice them. He was of marriageable age you see and every girl dreamt of becoming a princess by marrying him. He of course was used to this and it was more of an inconvenience than a benefit as he could never do the things he wanted to do without a crowd gathering. He liked fishing you see.

That and jousting.

He was fishing one day and he caught a big fish. He flipped it out onto the bank and the fish spoke to him. It asked to be set free as it didn't want to die. It was screaming as it had his hook in its mouth.

Marikus was proud of his catch. It was indeed a big fish. So he didn't want to let it go. He took his club and was about to kill the fish when there was a flash of light and the fish became a water nymph.

The water nymph was very angry. Quite understandably so. She then cursed Marikus and he became the beast that you see now. She then leapt back into the river.

The beast tried to catch her and he has been trying every since." Abigail looked at the beautiful woman. "So how come you married him? Was it because even though he was the beast you see he was a wonderful person underneath?"

The Witch shook her head. "He is not a wonderful person. He is vicious, angry, proud and selfish. I was promised to him when my father and his father signed a peace treaty. My father was unaware of the curse but he was bound by his promise.

I came to live here as the King would not tolerate his son in the palace.

He didn't want to see what he had become and when he lost his temper the strength of the beast is ore than the doors in the palace could contain.

So he built this house and we moved here. Now he spends his days looking out of the window or sitting by the stream trying to catch the nymph."

Abigail looked down into her cup. "So you are married to a man you do not love. That is sad. I don't think I could do that."

The Witch smiled kindly. "I hope that you never have to be in that position. I was a princess, that is what princesses do, they do their duty."

Abigail looked down at her shoes. They were no longer the pretty clean shoes she loved. They were battered and dirty from walking. Her white socks were mud stained and her dress was in tatters. She was about to speak up and say that she was a princess too but she decided not to. "Can we help?"

The Witch looked at the ornaments on the mantelpiece for something to look at. "I don't know. It was a water nymph's curse and I don't know how to break it."

Abigail looked at the pretty princess witch and tried not to look sad. "Well in stories the curses seem to be broken by a kiss or falling love with the beast."

The witch looked sad. "I have kissed him and I do love him, despite his grumpy ways. You get used to it after a while if you don't expect him to be nice."

Abigail looked around the room. "I don't know how you can break the curse as you must love him to put up with him."

The witch looked serious. "I have a feeling you are here as you think I can help you. So, in return perhaps you can help me. Would you go to the river and see if you can lure the river nymph out? Do you have something that she may be interested in?"

Abigail pulled out the bag and set the items out on the table. "I have these. Do you think that anything here would be of interest to her?"

The Witch picked up the small metal ornate bell. The sound it made was an ethereal tinkle and as she held it delicately between her fingers and looked at it she smiled. "This may just be the thing to get her to leave the water and step back onto land. Come with me, shall we go and find out?"

They left the room and walked down to the small stream which ran behind the house. There was a humped back bridge over it. One of those rough stone ones which always looks ancient.

The Witch went to the part of the river where there was a copse of trees. She looked around nervously and whispered. "Now if we hide in here quietly and if I can lure her out we can then leap out and catch her."

The Witch waited until they were all well hidden and the animals and birds had settled down. Gradually the normal sounds of nature returned and everything was still. Fluffy white clouds drifted aimlessly across the blue sky. The sun shone down. Butterflies fluttered. Birds flittered about looking for a meal. The plants grew unseen and the warmth of the sun on their face made Abigail almost forget what she was hiding in the trees for. Actually she didn't really know what they were going to do other than to catch the nymph.

The Witch rang the bell. It was a small sound but on a still day it was easy to hear it. The tinny, silvery sound was out of place and as she rang it again there was silence. Then she stopped ringing it and the silence was almost deafening.

They waited and waited. She rang it again as they intently watched the water. As they watched the water a fish's fin broke the surface. The fish was swimming around a small pool in the rocks, a deeper part of the river. Around and around it swam. Its fin broke the surface then its nose and then its mouth.

The Witch rang the bell again as the fish seemed to be losing interest and almost swam away. It then swam back and was back in the pool. Its fin broke the surface, its nose broke the surface and then the witch moved like lightning. Abigail didn't see her move but the next thing she saw was the Witch flipping the fish out of the water.

The fish landed on the bank and flapped furiously but the Witch had her foot on its large tail. It flapped and flapped and gasped for water. Its mouth was open wide and its eyes looked about in fear.

Abigail noticed that there was a large fish hook stuck in its mouth. Perhaps if we take the hook out of the fish it will forgive him and break the curse?

The Witch smiled. "You could be right." She reached down and held the fish with one hand and then pulled the hook from the fish's mouth.

The fish still flapped but not so furiously. It was exhausted and suffering from being out of the water.

The Witch looked down at the fish. "If you break the curse you put on my husband I will free you."

The fish opened and shut its mouth.

At that moment the beast came running from the house. As he ran he changed. The beast disappeared and a handsome man appeared. He was tall and thin and dashing. His black hair was long and his nails unkempt but he was still handsome. He was the Prince again.

He ran over to where they were and looked down at the fish. He then pulled his knife and cut the fish's head off with one stroke. "We will dine well tonight."

The Witch glared at him in horror. "But she broke the curse."

The ex beast shrugged. "So what, she is a fish. We will now eat the fish." He took the fish from the shocked wife and carried it to the house.

The Witch looked at Abigail in horror. "I didn't think he would do that."

She then followed him back to the house and Abigail and Lemmie followed as well.

They stood outside and they could hear the sound of raised voices inside. The Witch was shouting very loudly and then there was a loud explosion, a puff of green smoke and the Witch was heard laughing, or more likely cackling.

Abigail stood on tip toes and looked in through the window. The green smoke cleared and the Witch was standing in the middle of the kitchen and was just bending down to pick up a large toad which sat on the wooden floor looking stunned.

The Witch looked up and saw Abigail. "Come in, I won't hurt you."

Abigail and Lemmie walked in through the kitchen door. The room was still neat and tidy once the green smoke had cleared. All manner of copper pans hung from an airer over the range stove and the big wooden country kitchen table was clean and tidy.

The Witch sat down at the table and put the toad on a towel. "Sit down, don't worry, he won't hurt you either. He won't hurt anyone anymore. You are right, it is hard to live with someone like that. He was better as the beast as that kept him away from people and I could look after him here. He was a nasty and vain manipulative creature before he became the beast. As a toad he will be unable to harm anybody. No doubt plenty of women will hear the story and go around kissing toads looking for him and hoping to be made into Princesses but don't worry, nobody will find him."

Abigail hadn't realised that she was staring at the toad. "But you turned him into a toad."

The Witch smiled. "He always a toad, a mean and nasty toad. My magic is white magic, I cannot harm someone who is kind and good and my magic only does what it is necessary to do.

As a handsome man he would be able to return to his father. His father is a good and kind king. The son is a cruel and vicious spoilt brat who would in time grow to envy his father's position and wish to have his power. He wouldn't be able to wait for it as he has no patience or any love for his father. He has the ability to kill and his father would be in danger. Instead of a kind king and the benevolent rule of his younger son after his days are over we would have this creature on the throne. No, that cannot happen. So I turned him into a toad. Which is the last curse of the river nymph."

Abigail looked at the toad in horror. "But he is trapped in a toad's body now. Isn't that cruel?"

The Witch shook her head. "I am a white witch. He is not trapped in a toad's body, that would be cruel. He is a toad. As far as he knows he has always been a toad and he always will be a toad. There is nothing of the man in him left. I will now return him to the river bank and he will live his years out there."

Abigail looked at the slightly bedraggled witch. Her face was smutted by the green smoke which made her look like she had a green face. Her apron was patched with green. Her white dress was stained and she looked very tired and haggard. "Well what will happen to you?"

The Witch smiled. "Nothing will happen to me. I will go on living here. Now I must help you as you loaned me your bell." She gave Abigail her bell back and she put it back in the pouch. "You want to go home. To do that you will have to cross the dimensions and take yourself back to the time just before you eat the peach. Yes I know about the peach. You have to stop yourself doing it and then you will never have been here. But as time is not a straight line, all that you do here will remain done. So don't think that you can do what you like here."

Abigail looked puzzled. "So how do I cross the dimensions? Can you use your magic?"

The Witch shook her head. "No, that takes having a time machine. You will have to go and see the great wizard. He has machines like that. You have something in your favour though. That crystal in your bag is one of the crystals which powers his machine. I can draw you a map of how to get to him but you will have to pass through dangerous places to get there. But I think you have probably already guessed that."

Abigail nodded and looked down at Lemmie. "Yes, I had thought that it wouldn't be easy."

The Witch smiled. "Well you have one crystal but you will need others. You will have to go and see the woman who lives in the mountain with her small friends. They mine crystals like that which are used for power. If you can get some of their crystals then you will be able to use them to bargain with the wizard. But, they guard their crystals well and they do not trade with anyone.

The woman is very angry and spiteful as her family abandoned her to die. They tried to murder her. She doesn't trust royalty so I cannot come with you.

She is cursed that one day a Prince will come and she will be taken from her happy life and will have to go and take up the duties of being a Princess. So whatever you do make sure you do not mention that you are a Princess.

She loves sewing and makes all the clothes for her seven little friends. You have a thimble there, you may be able to trade that for what you want.

She lives just north of the wizened wood. Of course

getting through the wood won't be easy as it is full of wood nymphs. But you have something in your bag they will like, you have that other crystal in a pod. You may be able to trade that for safe passage. Or they may kill you.

Would you like more tea."

Abigail was stunned. "Yes please."

The Wood was dark and spooky. The undergrowth was thick, forcing them to zig zag to find their way through and the tree canopy blocked out most of the sunlight.

The undergrowth was like nothing Abigail had seen before. The bushes were strange black fungus like growths and the damp loam smelt of almonds.

This became sickening after a while as it was all she could smell.

The tree trunks were black and seemed to be coated with an oily substance and the boles in the trees were obviously occupied. Things moved in the periphery of her vision and things slithered out of her way in the distance. Black slug like creatures hung on the bushes, munching on the fibrous tendrils which made up the bushes.

The bear was back with them and the three of them walked closely together, looking from left to right, in front and behind.

In one of the tree trunk holes Abigail saw a tiny hand and big black eyes momentarily before they disappeared back inside.

Abigail was terrified and this wasn't helped as a black smoke swirled around her feet and then became solid in front of her. The smoke became a person. He person was dressed in a black cloak. All that could be seen was a pair of glowing red eyes.

She didn't know what to do then she remembered what the Witch had said. Her mind was racing as this couldn't be the wood nymph. She had imagined pretty wooden glades, rabbits skipping about and a unicorn or two. This dark and awful place could not be where a wood nymph lived. However she reached into the bag and took out the acorn like necklace and held it out to the creature.

The creature laughed and reached for it. Dark, oily, sinuous fingers reached for the trinket. Long clawed nails barely touched the necklace when there was a flurry of movement and a very loud. "Whoo hoo."

The black creature was knocked sideways by a large white horse which seemed to come from nowhere. The horse was ridden by what Abigail had always thought an elf would look like. Se was tall and thin. Her ears were archetype in that they were pointed.

Her gown was suitably diaphanous and her horse suitably noble, white with flowing feathered feet. As it landed with a snort, having knocked the black creature to the ground it pawed the ground with its hooves.

The elf reached down from the heady heights of the huge horse and snatched the trinket from the stunned Abigail's hand. "thank you, I think I'll take that. You want passage through the woodland, very well, go on and get on with it. Nothing will touch you, you have my word."

She then rode off, purposefully knocking the black creature over again as she went.

The dark creature got to his feet, dusted himself down and swore in a language that Abigail did not understand but she understood the tone. He then turned and faced her. "Oh well, it was pretty, thank you for the thought.

I wanted that but she always gets all the presents. Go on then, you are free to travel through the wood. Toll paid." He turned as if to go.

Abigail was stunned but she pulled herself around enough to be able to speak. "Who are you?"

The creature stopped and turned. "Well, you want to speak to me. That is amazing in itself. I am the spirit of the wood. This is the Heart of the Dark Wood from which all the greenery comes. Walk on a bit, you will come to the pretty green bit which I am sure you are here to see."

Abigail looked at the man, as the man was what he was. Like the elf, pointed ears, black robes which were now dirty. "You live here?"

The man smiled. "Don't be so derogatory of my home. Yes, I live here.

We live here. Me and my friends and family."

Abigail tried to hide her obvious surprise. "Forests are different where I come from."

The man laughed heartily. "There are forests and there are forests. This is a fungal forest which lives on the damp which is around here. To us it is beautiful. Like at those structures."

Abigail looked up with different eyes. She looked into the darkness and saw how the light cascaded through the sinuous canopy. This was truly magnificent. Like a huge stained glass window of intricate design. She looked at the bushes and instead of seeing something black and slimy she saw impossibly thin filaments which wove and twisted to make intricate natural designs like spun sugar.

Wherever she looked she saw an amazing world of

black and white. White marble rocks poked from the black loam. The light sparkled on the white quartz in a myriad of specs of colour.

The man smiled. "Now you are seeing it how someone who is unafraid sees it. That is the same as with many things. You see them as being ugly because you are afraid of them. If you look at the beauty of the night you will never be afraid of it."

Abigail looked down at her shoes again. "I was very afraid of the night and the garden at night."

The man smiled kindly. She could see his face now. It was a beautiful face, the face of an elf. "You fear then garden at night because it looks different What is there to be afraid of? That you would fall? That there would be wicked creatures there?

In a world like you come from. Yes I know your world. I don't like it but I know of it. What you fear is what might be lurking in the dark. Those are the things that man puts in the dark to scare himself. Nature didn't put them there. Nature is straightforward and you have killed off things that would naturally kill you in the dark. No more wolves hunt in packs. No more bears hunt for food. You live in a world where the greatest fear is man.

That is the best reason to fear the night or day. Our kind should have been terrified of you years ago, particularly those in your world. They have been driven to the fringes and almost destroyed."

Abigail shrugged. "I suppose so. I don't like the dark as I can't see what is hiding there."

The man smiled. "Why should there be anything hiding there? Does your fear put something there?"

Abigail smiled. "I suppose you are right. I fear the house at night too. It is noisy. Creatures crawl about. I can hear the floorboards moving."

The man looked down on her kindly. "When a tree is living it grows and it is silent. When she dies and is cut up to make a house she has a voice. A plank will make a noise if you step on it. It gets warm, its gets cold, it will make the same noise. Old houses settle at night. They creak and pipes make noises. You are making so much noise in the day that you don't notice them. At night when there are no noises you notice everything more. It is the same with the woodland.

The spirits of the woodland and houses have their own time. You are supposed to be in bed. As long as you stay where you should be then

everyone will be happy."

Abigail smiled. "You sound like my father."

The man laughed. "Well I'm someone's father. Not your father but a father to my children. You are trying to get home. How did you get here?"

Abigail's smile fell from her face. "I was a very naughty girl. My father had invented a machine which created a peach. I wanted the peach. So I sneaked into his laboratory and I eat the peach. Then tendrils came out of the peach stone and dragged me into the peach and here I am. So now I want to go home."

The man raised an eyebrow. "So you eat the proof that your father had succeeded in is experiment and before he could run tests on that peach to see if it was safe to eat. You are indeed a very naughty girl."

Abigail bit her lip. "I know and I am sorry. I just want to go home."

The man looked down at her. "I am sure that your father wants you home too. He will forgive you if you are sorry. If the machine made one peach it can make another. He only has one of you. He could make another but it wouldn't be you. So you must find your way home."

Abigail looked into her bag. There wasn't much left as she knew she had to keep the crystal and the thimble. "Does she always take the things you are given?"

The man smiled. "She is a Light Elf. They are used to gifts and expect everything to be theirs."

Abigail tipped the contents of the pouch into her hand and put them into her pocket. She then offered the man the bag. "Here, you should have something. Would you like the bag?"

The man took the bag. "Thank you, you are kind. Now you should go on your way. I hope you have learnt not to steal from your father and to listen to your parents."

Abigail and her friends walked on through the dark wood. It was far less frightening now and they passed the time spotting creatures which leapt, slithered and flittered away from them.

The path wound around trees and they had to jump three small streams. The black trees gradually became more green until they were walking in an idyllic sylvan woodland. The dark and slithery creatures became less. They were replaced by white rabbits, pretty birds and they caught sight of a pair of unicorns in the distance before they galloped off.

The squelchy loam of the dark wood became the firm lawn path of the light wood. The blackened bushes became the green fronds of ferns and the echoing silence transformed into the cacophony of twittering and animal sounds of the light wood.

The sun beamed down like little spotlights through the leafy tree cover. Insects filled the air. What looked like bees and butterflies flittered about their business, visiting the multicoloured flowers which lay like a carpet either side of the path.

The air smelt of the heady aroma of their scent. Floral with a hint of musk. The loam of the soil beneath adding its distinct damp aroma.

The path became longer grass and as they walked along Abigail ran her hands through it. Her fingertips ran over the blades as they pushed their way through.

Lemmie was trotting just behind her, bouncing over the taller grass and taking the odd bite as he went along. The bear as always walked slowly and silently behind them. He didn't say much, he just plodded on.

Small fair creatures were watching them. They could see them sitting on branches and in holes in the bowls of trees. They flew from branch to branch. Their gossamer wings carrying them effortlessly through the warm air.

It was noticeably warmer, noticeably brighter and noticeably prettier. The woodland looked manicured and planned, it didn't really look right to Abigail.

They walked on with caution. Abigail remembered an argument her parents had once had about whether fairies were good or evil, wicked or kind. Her mother had firmly put the argument that White Ladies, Knockers and Red Caps and other such creatures were not the benevolent creatures of fairy stories.

Each of those creatures could carry a poisoned needle or a magic spell. Any of them could dart in and kill them. So she sped up her step and the others fell in with her. She didn't want to talk about it but thoughts ran through her head. All the stories she had read in her mother's book came into her head. This was not a book for children as such, it was a guide to the fairy folk. As far as she had read, before she had put it back as she was too afraid, she had understood that they were wicked and there were very few, if any, who showed the benevolent ideas that she had read in fairy stories.

She focused on Tinkerbell. That good fairy. She focused on the Fairy Godmother and tried to put the other thoughts out of her mind. Her feet moved faster and they hurried their way through the woodland.

To their left there was a loud growl. The shadows moved and she saw what was making them move. A large brown bear stood up on its back legs and growled again.

As one Lemmie and Abigail leapt behind the very big

grey bear. He wasn't so small anymore. The grey bear stepped forwards and growled as well.

"Leave my friends alone!"

The bear dropped down onto four paws and sniffed the air. "You are in my territory."

Archie thought for a moment. "We are travelling through this woodland and following the path. We are not on your land, we are on the path or am I wrong?"

The bear shook himself. "You are not wrong. You are on a path. The path goes through my territory. I could still eat you. There are no rules about that sort of thing."

Archie shook his head, his fur flapping audibly against his body. "No, you cannot eat us. I will fight you if you try. You may win but you will be injured, that is certain. Injuries get infected so you may well die anyway. So I suggest that you let us pass."

The bear lifted a paw. "I am not hungry so you may go. Leave my land quickly before I change my mind."

They did, they almost ran for the next half of an hour until they hoped that they were out of the bear's territory.

The trees were still thick and a canopy of lush green. They walked on and on. Over hills, down gullies and then the trees and undergrowth started to thin out and they stepped out onto the foothills of a mountain range.

There was a single path which went up into the mountain. It was strewn with pebbles and rocks and looked as though it had been manmade as the rest of the terrain around it was covered in a thick carpet of grass.

They walked and walked, ascending as the path climbed higher and higher. The grass became noticeably thinner and rougher. The bushes thinned out until there were only small tufty bushes left that clung to the rough terrain. It became windier as well and noticeably colder. Abigail pulled her clothes around herself and plodded on.

She knew they were being watched. She could feel it and she saw the top of a red cap which was sticking up from behind a rock. "Hello, we are not here to harm you. We are travelers who want to carry on through the mountains."

They didn't move quickly but before Abigail and her friends could react they were surrounded by seven small men, each armed with picks. "You are our prisoners and we are going to take you to the boss. Walk in line and follow the first of us."

Abigail went first, she followed the first man and the others followed on behind. In her mind's eye she could see the picks, sharp and businesslike in the men's hands and she remembered the Witch's warning.

She kept quiet and they just walked in silence until they came to a cottage which was nestled in a flat part of the rock. Like the Witch's Cottage it was immaculate and pretty. The stonework was carved into intricate patterns and the windows were hung with neat curtains inside. Instead of the flowers there were mosses and rough grasses which had been arranged to grow like any ordinary beautiful garden. Interspersed amongst them there were stone statues of what Abigail would have called Garden Gnomes.

The boundary of the garden was set by a low white wall. The gate had two garden gnomes on guard. They were just like the one that her father had given to her mother. They were brightly coloured and their beards and hair were depicted as neatly cut and they were all the same size and shape. Each of them wore a hat which was identical all but for its colour. Each of them was depicted as wearing a jacket, waistcoat and a pair of trousers tucked into their black boots.

Abigail was led to the door by her guard. She approached the door and it opened. A middle aged woman stepped outside. She had long black hair which was smoothly brushed and kept in place with a red ribbon tied in a bow which she wore like a hairband. Her dress was a strong colour blue and yellow, the most noticeable feature being her puffed sleeves which were dual coloured in the same colours. She was beautiful but she looked angry. "Who are you and why are you on the mountain?"

Abigail remembered what the Witch had said. "We are travelers and I am looking for my way home. We mean you no harm."

The woman nodded. "Where is your home?"

Abigail was now a little lost for words. "My home is far from here, in another dimension. I need to find the wizard to be able to use his machine to go home. So I need some crystals from this mountain. I do not want to steal them, I would like to buy some if I can't find any."

The woman looked serious. "Oh you do, do you? Well they do not come cheap. If you have a sob story then you are probably looking for a good deal on what you are hoping to buy. Remember, we don't have to sell you anything. What do you have that we could possibly want?"

Abigail thought for a moment. "I have a magic thimble that will help you while you sew."

The woman looked at Abigail and laughed. "No you don't. You have an ordinary thimble and you want to pretend that it is magic to get a better deal.

Now, that is not the way to behave. I would be happy to have an ordinary thimble. I need one, that is enough. You don't need to pretend or make a story up. I know that you are a child and to you saying that something is magic is not as important as it really is. You are telling an untruth aren't you? You are telling me a lie. That is not acceptable in any creature, not least a child. Don't think that it is. If you are going to grow into a good adult you will have to learn to always tell the truth and to feel bad about even thinking about telling a lie.

I could punish you by telling you to go away and that you are a nasty little liar. I won't on this occasion if you promise never to lie again. Do you promise that?"

Abigail looked down at her dirty shoes and felt very, very small. "I promise."

The woman smiled. "Your word is your bond. If you break that promise then I will send a crow in your sleep to peck your eyes out. Is that a good incentive?"

The short men were all laughing heartily with their hands over their mouths.

Abigail was shocked. She had not expected that. "You can't say that!

You really can't say that. That is horrible! Do you mean it?"

The woman smiled wickedly. "Try it and find out. Now, show me the thimble. If I like it I will let you have a crystal."

Abigail put her hand into her pocket and took out the medieval style thimble. It was like a modern one but there was no top on it. It was more like a band or a ring. She put it in the woman's outstretched hand.

The woman laughed. "It is a very unusual thimble. I would like it so I will give you a crystal. Just so that you will appreciate the importance of what I am offering you I am going to send you to get it with my friends here. You are going to go down the mine and help them to bring back your crystal.

What do you think of that?"

Abigail looked surprised. "I don't know. I've never been into a mine. Is it dangerous?"

The woman laughed. "Of course it is. You could die going to get that crystal. But, my friends take that risk all the time. Why should they have to risk their life so you can swap a crystal for a thimble? You will go and get your own crystal."

The little goat bleated. "Do I have to go too?"

The woman smiled kindly at the little goat. "No, you are too small and your hooves wouldn't be very secure down the mine. You would have to climb ladders and you cannot do that. You can stay here with me and eat grass and plants around my house if you like."

The little goat looked worried. "I don't know. When I'm away from my friend would you do something horrible to me?"

The woman laughed. "Why are you worried about something like that.

With your friend the bear there, not a chance."

Abigail looked and felt nervous as she walked cautiously down the rubble strewn tunnel which sloped sharply down into the blackness of the earth.

It wasn't completely dark. With just a flick of light the world came to life. Tiny creatures and plants took that light and began to glow. All around her the world was a wondrous mix of colours glowing and moving around. Some moved slowly, for example the snail like creatures. Some moved remarkably fast, they were like butterflies. They landed on the mosses and ferns which grew in the dark.

Abigail was mystified by their ability to live without

light. Then she thought it through. She was in a different world and things here were different. Why would she assume they would be the same as in her world? They must be living on something but whatever it was it was definitely not sunshine. She had not seen the sun now for over half an hour.

The ground was slightly damp, a rivulet of water ran down the middle of the tunnel floor. It had cut a "v" shaped groove into the rock and wove its way around the fixed lumps which protruded from the ground.

Abigail was in the middle of the group of men. In front of her was a particularly grumpy one who kept moaning that she was walking too close to him. Behind her the nearest short man kept sneezing. At first it made her jump but then she got used to it.

The short man who was leading the group began singing and seemed to love every step of the journey.

They strode on, their tiny lanterns lit the way. She then noticed that each lantern had a glowing worm in it which glowed brightly enough to light their way. They didn't need much light as what little light they brought with them seemed to set off a cascade of light which rolled off into the distance to light their way. She was stunned at first but she soon got used to it. It was beautiful, like a wave of colour that faded into the darkness in front of her, making it less threatening.

Multicoloured fibrous fronds hung down from the ceiling. They wafted as the air moved, caused by their movement along the tunnel. Hair like moss hung down, making the ceiling look like fur. It waved and undulated as she passed along under it. The fronds seemed so delicate that any kind of movement in the air moved them.

One of the subterranean butterfly creatures landed on the end of one of the hair like fronds. She jumped as a spike shot from the depths, impaling the butterfly before pulling it into the soft bed of fronds. In the middle of such beauty such sudden death shocked her.

The short man in front of her had turned at that point and saw her watching the plant hunting. "Don't reach up by the way, those things will kill you. They have the deadliest poison known to dwarf."

Abigail put her hands in her pockets. "Don't worry, I do not intend to.

They look so beautiful though."

The Dwarf grunted and carried on down the tunnel which went on and on. It was descending, down and down. Then it ended in a sheer drop. The others stopped before the drop so she didn't need to worry other than looking down made her feel dizzy.

One by one they climbed onto the ladder which was tied to the wall and began climbing down. This was something she definitely did not want to do. She could see it was a long way down, or rather she couldn't. The ladder descended into the darkness. Illuminating fronds lit up as they descended and as she passed them and the air became still again their light went out above. She could see that the hole was about fifty feet in diameter.

Nervously she counted the steps, using the numbers to focus her thoughts. She passed five hundred and began to panic.

The fronds and other plants had been cut back away from the ladder to keep their poisonous spines away from those who climbed cautiously down. The cut back area was a distinct dark spine descending into the darkness.

Abigail passed a ledge which had a pile of stones on it. She passed another and another. She had to ask. "What are these piles of stones for?"

The dwarf who was above her sneezed and answered when he had recovered his composure. "Each of us has their own ledge. We keep stones on there that we have found and liked. Don't touch them please." He then sneezed again and carried on climbing down.

Abigail smiled. She liked that idea.

Then they came to the bottom of the ladder. The tube opened up into a small cavern which was also illuminated by fronds but also by lanterns. These came to light as the dwarves tapped them and woke up the worms that lived in them. One by one the grumpy one went to the pole and put some food in it from a pouch he carried on his belt. As he fed them they glowed brighter.

There were five tunnels heading away from the cavern and each was illuminated into the distance. They all looked the same.

One of the dwarves set off down one of them. Abigail followed in silence.

She had questions but she didn't want to ask at the moment.

Everything echoed oddly and her feet made splashing noises in the pools of liquid on the floor which made the rock look slippery. She then realised that the pools were oil, not water. Rainbow colours swirled around the surface and clung to her shoes.

On and on they went along the tunnel. They traveled for a while before it opened out into a huge cavern.

As the stepped into the cavern sparkles of light filled her field of vision. As she stepped into the darkened cavern the pinpoints of light looked like a night sky.

As they stepped in and aggravated the fronds they illuminated and she could see the cavern better.

Huge bunches of crystals clustered together around the ceiling, walls and floor. One tiny point reflected and bounced between the crystals, magnified and the cavern was then lit.

One of the dwarves walked over to Abigail. "Well Abigail, here you are. You will need four of these crystals to power the device for the mage. We trade with him often so we know what is needed. You have already traded for one. He will trade for two and you will need to use two. You must promise never to tell anyone what you have seen. Our lady will bind you to that promise. By the way, don't think that she won't."

Abigail's mouth was open. She closed it. "I promise. I won't tell anyone but this is beautiful. Why is she so threatening? She doesn't seem nice at all."

The dwarf smiled. "She hasn't had a good life. Her mother died and her father remarried. Her stepmother is a beautiful woman and was jealous of our lady. She tried to murder her but she escaped into the woods. We found her when she was lost and alone and we decided to keep her. She is useful after all. She has lived with us for many years.

She is very friendly with the Witch who lives in the valley and the Witch can tell fortunes. Her fortune is to marry a Prince so eventually she would become a Queen. That is a heavy burden for her to carry. One day she will have to leave us behind and go to live in an elaborate palace where she will have to mind her manners, always dress perfectly and be responsible for all manner of difficult situations. She would be watched, whatever she does and she will have to do official visits rather than what she wants to do. She will have to make huge decisions that will effect people's lives and have to be responsible when things go wrong.

We arte also at war with the neighouring country of Llarrkkenvolm. If she is Queen she will have to make decisions which will send many of our people to die for their country.

She wants to stay here. She wants to enjoy her life and her sewing. But she knows one day she will have to leave. So that is hanging over her every day and that doesn't make her happy.

Also, she knows that her father doesn't know how wicked his new wife is. She has redesigned the castle and thrown out everything that was her mother's. She sometimes hears about what is going on and although her father is happy, his new wife is domineering and he has very little to say.

It is because of her that the country is at war. Our lady firmly believes that.

Our lady has learnt magic from the Witch and she has learnt lots of other things for when she does have to go back. One day her prince will come. I think she part dreads it, part looks forward to it. For now, she is as happy here as she can be with that hanging over her."

Abigail looked puzzled. "Why wouldn't she want to live in a palace, be pampered and wear beautiful things?"

The dwarf shook his head. "You didn't listen to a word I said did you? Being a princess is more than wearing pretty clothes and having people do things for you. They do things for you so that you can have time to do all those jobs that nobody in their right mind would want to do. Would you like to be responsible for everyone in this country? Would you like to make decisions that could send them to their death?"

Abigail frowned. "Well no, actually I wouldn't. I never thought of it that way."

The dwarf smiled. "Don't worry, not many people do. Well we'd better get you your crystals and you can be on your way." He saw Abigail's sad look. "What is the matter? You'll be home sooner than you think."

Abigail looked down at the floor. "I like it here in this world, it is magical and amazing."

The dwarf shook his head. "You are here in the summer, you would not like it when the veil of white comes down over the world."

Abigail smiled. "I bet it looks amazing."

The dwarf sighed. "The optimism of youth. Come on then, we will get your crystals."

Abigail was thoughtful as she climbed back up the ladder. Her arms ached, her legs ached and she was tired.

Back at the Cottage the little goat was playing with the woman. As soon as Abigail had left the woman had relaxed and found him carrots. The bear was laid out on a rock sunning himself. They ran around and around. First the goat was chasing, then the woman. Then they collapsed in the sun, looking out over the amazing view they could see from their elevated position in the mountains. The woman absentmindedly stroked the goat who was laid out enjoying the sun.

As they saw Abigail making her way down the mountain on the narrow goat track towards them they got up. The woman dusted herself off and the waited for the group of Abigail and the dwarves to arrive.

Abigail was quiet when she got back to the Cottage. She smiled at the woman. "It is beautiful down there. Where was the danger?"

The woman smiled. "There is danger in all things. If you are careful the danger doesn't matter. Danger is only important if it is relevant to you. Well you had better go now before it gets dark. It is difficult in these mountains in the dark."

Abigail and her friends made their way along the mountain path that the woman had suggested. They were very careful and watched their feet every step of the way. When they wanted to look at the scenery they stopped in a good place and just looked.

A few miles saw them out of the mountains and into a small wood where they decided to stay the night. It was warm so there was no need for blankets or a house. The sky was slightly overcast with cloud so it did not get colder as the sun went down.

They slept and were not woken. Even when the denizens of the woodland came to look. They didn't bother them. Their long arms were kept in their pockets. Their hoods were kept up over their pointed heads and pointed ears. They didn't steal and they didn't murder. They had no reason to. They saw the travelers and they were not hungry and neither did they need anything that the travelers looked like they had. So they had a look, had a sniff and went away.

Abigail and her friends woke up in the morning refreshed.

They got up and started walking again, following the directions that the woman had given them. They knew what to expect so when they came to a tower they were not surprised. It rose up from the plain. It looked huge and imposing, even from the distance when they first saw it and it was a long way away then.

It got bigger as they got closer and as they did they felt smaller. They knew the could be seen. There was nowhere to hide. The plain was just grass, no bushes, no trees. They walked through a sea of green.

Nearer and nearer they came and as they came to the big wooden door at its base it swung open. This made Abigail jump as she had just been reaching for the door knocker. A voice boomed out. "Enter travelers." They did.

The room beyond was created from glowing white marble which had a silver thread running through it. It had no safety rail and looked slippery. They had no choice, they had to step inside and as they did the door slammed shut behind them. The voice boomed out again. "Sorry, slipped. Come up the stairs."

They then saw the stairs. They were against the far wall. As they climbed the staircase went up to higher levels but someone was in the room waiting for them so they stepped off onto the floor of the circular room above.

There was nothing in the room other than a sofa and two chairs, a fire which was suspended in the air with no fireplace or flue, a coffee table and on it a pot of tea and cups set out neatly on a tray.

Sitting in one of the armchairs they could see a thin man. He was unremarkable in all ways. His hair was short but not too short. His nose was slightly pointed, but not too pointed. His round glasses were poised on the end of his nose and as he saw them he pushed them back into place. He didn't look much like a wizard in Abigail's opinion. There were no robes and no pointed hat. He looked like the boy down the road who she had known for years and he too would have worn a hand knitted jumper and chino trousers.

He looked up. "Hello Abigail. So you want to go home?"

Abigail was stunned. "Well, yes. I have crystals, two for you, two to work your device."

The man shrugged. "Very good, put them down on

the table. Would you like a cup of tea? Forgive me but I don't get many visitors. I have got sugar and milk, do you like those?"

The mage made them a cup of tea and Abigail sat on the sofa. The little goat sat down beside her on the floor and the bear crouched down and sat beside the goat.

The man looked uncomfortable. "I am not used to this sort of a situation. I expect you are not used to it either. You want to go home. I got a message from my friend the Witch so I know this. You have the payment. So I can send you home now. We will finish our tea and I will arrange it." He seemed distracted. He was hardly looking at them and seemed to be bored by the situation.

Abigail drank her tea slowly. Her head was full of thoughts and she was glad of the silence. The man drank his tea too and seemed to be looking at the book that was open on the arm of his chair.

Abigail recognised the book. It was a school science book she had seen her neighbour with. It seemed odd to her but she didn't want to ask.

She looked at the little goat at her side. She looked at the big bear who sat looking around the room and she thought. I don't see them again! If I go home I will never see them again. Her hand reached out and she stroked the little goat who looked up at her with his big brown eyes. "I don't know if I want to go home. I like it here."

The mage looked up. "Of course you want to go home . It is why you took your journey and you do not belong here."

Abigail looked sad. "Can I visit?"

The wizard laughed. "Of course you cannot visit. You don't belong here. So I'm going to send you home. You have drunk the tea. You will now go to sleep here and wake up back at home. Say goodbye to your friends."

Abigail looked horrified. She grabbed little goat up onto her lap and cuddled him. He licked her face and nuzzled her neck. She hugged bear but as she was hugging him she felt her arms go through him. He was no longer there.

She was laying in her own bed in her own room. She could see the wallpaper she knew so well. She could see the animals and trees. She could see her toys. There was her little brown fluffy goat in its basket. There was her grey bear on its shelf with its green material bottle of champagne. Her picture of Snow White and the Seven Dwarfs was on the wall over her shelf.

She was home.

Her mother and father were sitting beside her. As her eyes opened they had looked at each other in relief then smiled at her.

"Welcome back little one. We were very worried about you."

Abigail cried. She cried more than she had ever cried in her life. She didn't want to be home, however much she loved her parents. She wanted to be in the world of magic where everything was different. She didn't want to go to school after the Christmas Holiday. She didn't want to sit at dinner and enjoy that wonderful meal. She didn't want her presents. She just wanted to go back to a world where everything was magical.

But she was home.

THE END